PARACHUTE

Focusing on novels with contemporary concerns, Bantam New Fiction introduces some of the most exciting voices at work today. Look for these titles wherever Bantam New Fiction is sold:

WHITE PLACE by Glenn Savan
SOMEWHERE OFF THE COAST OF MAINE by Ann Hood
COYOTE by Lynn Vannucci
VARIATIONS IN THE NIGHT by Emily Listfield
LIFE DURING WARTIME by Lucius Shepard
THE HOLLOWEEN BALL by James Howard Kunstler
PARACHUTE by Richard Lees

THUNDER ISLAND by James Howard Kunstler (on sale in May)
WAITING TO VANISH by Ann Hood (on sale in June)
BLOCKBUSTER by Douglas G. McGrath and Patricia Marx (on sale in July)
GOOD ROCKIN' TONIGHT by William Hauptman (on sale in August)
SLIGHTLY LIKE STRANGERS by Emily Listfield (on sale in September)
LOSS OF FLIGHT by Sara Vogan (on sale in October)

BANTAM NEW FICTION

PARACHUTE

RICHARD LEES

BANTAM BOOKS
TORONTO • NEW YORK • LONDON • SYDNEY • AUCKLAND

PARACHUTE
A Bantam Book / April 1988

Grateful acknowledgment is made for permission to reprint the following excerpts, "Burning Down the House," copyright © 1983 BLEU DISQUE MUSIC CO., INC. & INDEX MUSIC. All rights administered by WB MUSIC CORP. All rights reserved. Used by permission. "Miss You," copyright © 1978 by EMI MUSIC PUBLISHING LTD. All rights for the U.S. and Canada controlled by COLGEMS-EMI MUSIC INC. "My City Was Gone," words and music by Chrissie Hynde. Copyright © 1982 CLIVE BANKS MUSIC LIMITED. All rights controlled and administered by APRIL MUSIC INC. Under license from ATV MUSIC (WELBECK). All rights reserved. International copyright secured. Used by permission. "Everywhere That I'm Not," copyright © 1982 by VERY SAFE MUSIC & SLEEPLESS MUSIC. Used by permission of Warner-Tamerlane Publishing Corp. All rights reserved. "Sun King," words and music by John Lennon & Paul McCartney. Copyright © 1969 NORTHERN SONGS LIMITED. All rights reserved for the U.S.A., Canada, and Mexico controlled and administered by BLACK-WOOD MUSIC INC. Under License from ATV (MACLEN). All rights reserved. International copyright secured. Used by permission. "Jeopardy," written by Greg Kihn & Steve Wright. Copyright © 1983 by RYE BOY MUSIC/WELL RECEIVED MUSIC. "Every Breath You Take" by Sting. Copyright ILLEGAL SONGS, INC. Used by permission. Mark Strand, excerpted from THE STORY OF OUR LIVES. Copyright © 1973 by Mark Strand. Reprinted with the permission of Atheneum, an imprint of Macmillan Publishing Company. "Should I Stay or Should I Go?" copyright © by Nineden Ltd., London.

Library of Congress Cataloging-in-Publication Data

Lees, Richard.
  Parachute.

  I. Title.
PS3562.E3728P37 1988 813.54 87-47802
ISBN 0-553-34510-9 (pbk.)

Published simultaneously in the United States and Canada

Bantam Books are published by Bantam Books, a division of Bantam Doubleday Dell Publishing Group, Inc. Its trademark, consisting of the words "Bantam Books" and the portrayal of a rooster, is Registered in U.S. Patent and Trademark Office and in other countries. Marca Registrada. Bantam Books, 666 Fifth Avenue, New York, New York 10103.

PRINTED IN THE UNITED STATES OF AMERICA
FG   0   9   8   7   6   5   4   3   2   1

For Carol

Lynnie,

I know we haven't spoken much lately. And it's odd that I can write what I've been unable to say to your face. But if I guessed right, you've just gotten into bed and discovered this, which means I come to you in a way—with words—and at a time—at night—when you need me most.

I know you share my hopes for this trip. And I could tell by the look in your ocean eyes last night that you share my fears. We've waited a long time for this moment. Through all the years, all the travels, all the little productions in little towns' little theaters with little minds to miss the little things, you've been right there with me waiting and hoping for New York. I remember when we left New Haven after the Drama School, the way you looked at me in the hot asphalt parking lot of that Big Boy's as we were about to climb in the Ryder and head west. "Are you sure?" you wanted to know. "As long as I'm with you," I answered. And I meant it. Just as I mean it now.

Maybe it's taken all this time for a reason. Maybe I was lucky to be allowed my mistakes out in the bush. If so, fine. But I'll tell you, I've never felt more ready to leave anything behind in my life. I only hope that these people are as serious as they claim to be, because this play in my pocket *belongs* in New York.

So as I climb into the sky and you climb into bed, let's toast the new year as our own and resolve to make it so. Maybe our time has arrived. God, I hope so. I don't think I've ever wanted anything so much—except maybe you.

You take care of yourself and keep that duggie close by. She's amazingly good at warding off the phantoms in the night. I'll call you from Central Park West. (The guy has to have real money to live there, right? This thing is going to happen!) Keep warm and stay cool. I'm on my way to the Big Apple, where I intend to be nobody's fool.

All my heart, all my love, all the time,
your JJ

My JJ,

Well, you're on your way. If I planted this properly, you should be well into the flight as well as your second gin and tonic, and you've just decided the pilot knows what he's doing enough to take your eyes from your port look-out, and you've surveyed who is around you and who you can't take your eyes off of, and you've flirted with the stews enough to get your third G&T when you need it, and now you reach down to your duck bag and check out your wallet, your ticket, your *Tennis* magazine, and your notebooks, and you lean back, adjust the seat, and think, hey, wait a minute, what was that, and you bend back down to the duck bag, open it again, reach in for the notebook, the leather-covered one, and what do you know, you find me.

Forgive me for opening the notebook. I closed my eyes when I did it, held it just long enough to slip this note in. I had to say a few things, JJ, and I don't have to tell you it hasn't been easy to talk to you lately. Besides, I figure what can you do from 30,000 feet that the third G&T isn't going to take care of anyway?

First, I'm so proud of you. This is it, Mr. Playwright. You finally get a chance to strut your stuff for the big boys. I've known since that very first note you put in my pocket back in Ann Arbor (the one with the little triangles on it) that this day would arrive. It was just a matter of time and patience, both of which you've had more than your share of while you waited, while *we* waited. But, JJ, it's finally here, and I'm so glad it's with this play. This play belongs in New York. It reeks of New York. It's going to make you in New York.

And Futterman has to be for real. He wouldn't be flying you in and putting you up in his place if he weren't. (After all, this isn't the movies. . . .) He obviously knows a good thing when he sees it and he's just lucky enough to have seen you. Hopefully the changes he'll want won't be enormous and you'll be able to do them in time to get the play on in the fall like you said.

So, enjoy yourself, my love. You could use a break from things here anyway and I know how much you love New York by yourself. It's funny, I still feel guilty sometimes that you're not there, like it was my fault that we moved to California when you belong back east. But it does make for these trips and you never fail to come away from them with a play or a story or more. Who knows if it would be the same with us living there?

So go ahead, and know that me and Duggie Whitefoot are fine here holding down the fort. We love you and miss you, but our hearts are with yours, in the play. Be good, do good, and stay warm somehow. Show them a California boy can make it in a city that never sleeps.

I am your love, my love. Always.
Lynnie

4

PETER FUTTERMAN

JJ—

Good morning. I hope you slept off some of your jet lag and are ready to take on New York City today.

Susie and I have still one more New Year's brunch to do and expect to be gone most of the afternoon. Here is a little something to warm your pocket—enjoy your first meal here on your producer. I've arranged for you to meet with Maggie Steinfeld tomorrow and then we can all look forward to getting into bed on this project.

Stay warm and make yourself comfortable around the apartment. We're glad to have you with us. See you later.

Peter

Lynn Towne
8541 Coldwater Canyon
Los Angeles, CA 90056

Lynnie—

It's a gorgeous Sunday here. Ice cold but with a bright winter sun gleaming on everything. Remember when we used to go out for breakfast on days like this back in Ann Arbor and New Haven? There's something about bundling up in a Bean shirt, jeans, scarf, and gloves, and a good winter jacket, and then peeling it all off over a steaming cup of coffee while you wait for an omelet in a noisy restaurant. . . .

It was a good week. I had three long sessions with Maggie Steinfeld and she impresses me. She's quick and smart and knows what this play is about. She talks more in generalities than I'm used to from a director, but it's kind of nice to think someone might have more on her mind than setting light levels and blocking patterns. She does do a lot of drugs though. In fact, everyone here does. It's funny to me because you know how all the talk always has LA walking around stoned? Well, I'll tell you, I've never seen people smoke so much dope as I have here in the last five days. Right after breakfast or walking down a street. You get offered a joint, it seems, the minute you get out of bed. Everyone is high all the time. It's like the whole city is hyped and speeding and consuming drugs the way it consumes everything else—at an unbelievable fever pitch.

Anyway, we *have* had some great talks about the

6

play. Maggie's as eager as I am, and if it's not all a pipe dream, I think I'm in good shape. Futterman likes our ideas and seems anxious to get it on. He asked me how long I thought the rewrites would take because he's apparently already talking to investors. We're going to meet with Dianne Aimsley this week too. She's hungry, and according to Futterman thinks this sounds like a great part to an actress gone from the stage for too long. Nothing like people involved in a project for selfish reasons, right? They're the ones you can count on. But we shall see. . . . I don't want to get too far ahead of myself. I do have some work to do.

Which brings me to the next thing. It's working out so well with me here in the apartment and all, that Futterman has offered to let me stay instead of going home to do the writing. We all think it might speed things along, as I would have the benefit of immediate feedback, etc. I know we didn't have that in mind, but I think I may take him up on the offer. The way I look at it, I want to do whatever I have to do to make this happen as soon as possible. Also, let's face it, when am I going to have my own room on Central Park West in the foreseeable future? Even if it is covered in paisley and has no door. And did I tell you? In addition to the yellow paisley on electric-blue walls, there are also bizarre black wood sculptures of Futterman and his wife nude that look like life-size voodoo fetish dolls. His even has horns on the head. Nice room for me to work in, huh? How about sleep in?

It's taking some "adjustment," shall we say, but I do look out on a spectacular view of the city every night and all those lights seem to tell me that my dreams could come true. I miss you, Lynnie, but I think I'm going to stay. Unless I can't write away from my desk. And the only way I'll know that is to try.

I hope you're doing okay there by yourself. Are you

sleeping all right? Feeling all right? What's going on at work?

I think I'll call you soon. I need the sound of your voice in my ear for real. It's funny, I sometimes think I hear you when I'm in the shower. Aural hallucination. Or aural sex. Did I ever tell you how I love the music of your voice? I think I'll call you right now, in fact. I feel the approach of the tattered ghost of frustration.

I love you, my love.
JJ

Sunday night, January 8

Mr. J. J. Towne
c/o Futterman
183 Central Park West
New York, NY 10023

Dear JJ,

That was such a nice call, I just had to write you. I started
a letter to you this morning, but I was in such a weird
mood that I ended up throwing it away. You know Sun-
days have never been my favorite thing out here, even
with you around. Everyone seems jumpy, like they're
supposed to be happy with the bright sun shining, and the
fact that they're really alone and frightened, like Sunday
people everywhere, may not survive the day a secret
intact. But I will, right? Now that I've talked to you, the
demons have dissolved.

Of course, stay there. I absolutely agree. You'd be
crazy not to, and believe me, I'll be fine. Rudi's the best
company in the world. In fact, I kind of like the way she
becomes mine when we're alone here. She stays closer to
me, cuddles more, and likes to watch when I take a bath
or put on my makeup. She's more of a girl. Don't worry,
she'll abandon me the minute you walk back in the house,
but for now I'll glory in the attention. You stay there and
do what you have to do.

I'm glad you feel so comfortable with the city now (if
not with your paisley den and fetish dolls . . .). I remember when New York used to intimidate you, even when
we were in New Haven. Don't be afraid to go with your
instincts, JJ. They haven't gotten you into anything you've

9

regretted yet. And most important, do what's right for the play. If this works out the way it's sounding, we'll have all the time together we could ever want. We'll be sipping margaritas with Deek in Malibu, or better yet with Dianne Aimsley on her boat down in Barbados. I liked that story about the note in the bottle telling her an opportunity was coming her way. Do you think it's really true or was it the actress spinning a good yarn?

I love you a lot and it's fun to think of you with all these people. It's where you belong, JJ. So just enjoy it, okay? I'm going to bed now, where I intend to dream about you until I can feel you inside me, where I can always feel you, where I can surround your love with my own until there is no distance between us, where the difference between sleep and love is a secret I lay on your pillow and hold close to me all through the night.

I am yours always,
Lynnie

Sunday, January 8, 1 AM

I am now alone. JJ has left me. And not just to go to New York, like we've pretended. People who stop talking pretend all kinds of things, the main one being that they're not pretending. But I know better. This time I think it's for real. I heard it in his voice when he asked me how I was doing without him. Fine, I said, across the longing of long distance. And fine I must be. He is becoming the person he's always wanted to be. The one for whom there will be no me.

And so tonight I start this journal because I must have a home for my thoughts. Funny, the idea of a home for thoughts. I wonder if the truth can live even there.

11

Wednesday, January 11

Mr. J. J. Towne
c/o Futterman
183 Central Park West
New York, NY 10023

Dear JJ,

How you doing in Fat City, my friend? I had lunch with
Lynn yesterday and she tells me you're hanging with the
crème de la crème. So tell me, huh? I'm starving for
images of the IRT. Or is that beneath you these days?
You're probably cruising Fifth Avenue in limos, right? As
long as you're not sipping G&T's at the Surf Club, I'll
basically swallow about anything. . .

We're into a gorgeous January. Haven't seen a cloud
since before Christmas, so my film is actually a day ahead
of schedule. The geniuses changed my favorite scene the
other day though. Remember how I had my hero see
himself in a mirror when he finally sleeps with the girl
he's obsessed with and it's the sight of him having sex
with her and not the sex that he gets off on? Well, somebody in the studio decided that the American public isn't
ready yet for a man to look at himself in a mirror during
sex. They want it to happen with the two of them in a car
and their reflection in a store window. I guess I shouldn't
complain, as this is the only serious change so far, but I
do sometimes wonder why I agreed to get involved with
this. Why didn't I just let them buy the book and go my
merry way, do you remember? Me either, but I think it's
what I'm about to do.

I actually started the novel I've been telling you about

the other day. I was reading outside as the sun was going down and I heard this crying sound. I wandered down on the beach to see what it was and it turned out to be a dolphin—or a killer whale, as my neighbor the migration expert later told me. Seems some of them get lured by the warm currents here and separate from the rest of the school, and, being monogamous, they cry out for their mates to join them. Well, it's quite a sound, and I took it as a sign because it gave me my first line, and you know what happens with me once I get the first line. I'm off and running and I think my attitude toward the film is that much better as a result. I've always preferred indifference as a defense. When it's sincere, it gives such a feeling of being in sync with the universe. . .

I guess that's about it from Lotusland. Seriously, write me. I'd love to hear how it's going. Lynn looked great, by the way. If you don't come back soon, I may have to take advantage of a certain look I detected in those luscious green eyes of hers.

Best, as always,
Deek

Saturday, January 14

Lynn Towne
8541 Coldwater Canyon
Los Angeles, CA 90056

Dear Lynnie,

Hi. Got your Sunday letter yesterday. What a difference a call makes, huh? I wish you'd just pick up the phone when you're feeling that way instead of letting it go on. But sometimes I think you enjoy that kind of suffering. At least on some level. I'm not criticizing. I do, too, as long as it doesn't last too long. I don't know, there's something about loneliness after you've been together as long as we have that seems to restore the soul. Almost like you need it in order to feel your heart again. Maybe we should open a business: Loneliness Tours, a vacation in isolation for the very married, we give you the absence, you let your heart grow fonder. . . Probably make a fortune in LA. Or anywhere for that matter.

Anyway, I'm glad you're okay now. Me too. I'm feeling great, in fact. Saw some old friends this week—Bill and Marge, Alan, Steve-o, and even Jingles walking up Columbus Avenue in the middle of a perfectly ordinary afternoon. He's finally doing lighting design for a couple of theaters, so he's pretty happy. Everyone else is about the same, still fighting the good fight and looking for a way to make it pay. Sixties outcasts in the Land of Yup. They all send love.

Looks like we may have a fifth party involved in the play now too. Dot Penner, the soap actress on *Down by the River* who produced *Day Care* off-Broadway last

14

year. (Remember that? We read a lot about it in *The Times*.) Anyway, she and Maggie are old friends, so Maggie gave her a copy of the script to read and she had so much to say about it that Futterman invited her in on the deal. I guess he's secure enough to share the limelight with anyone who can help us get to it. I like her personally, since she's fun on top of being smart. Maggie does get a little dour after you've been in a room with her for seven hours, so maybe Dot will liven things up a bit. She plays this really funny southern belle on the soap and she slips into her voice just when everyone needs a laugh. Also she lives with Sevi Paretti's brother and he's producing films these days, so our night life is picking up as well. They get decent tables in restaurants.

That's about it. We're going out to dinner, so I have to hit the shower. I bought my yellow paper this afternoon and cleared a table in Futterman's den. I start the new draft Monday morning. Wish me luck.

Talk to you soon.

Love you.
JJ

Saturday, January 14, 11:46 PM, Melon's, NYC

Andee—

I'm right, aren't I? We're going to want to remember the time and place we first met? If you think so, too, keep this. And call me. Dot has the number.

JJ

Mr. Richard Case
27 Saltair Road
Malibu, CA 90233

Dear Deek,

Thanks for the letter. Glad to hear the movie's rolling and
that you're starting to divorce yourself from it. From where
I sit, that sounds like the best of both worlds. You're a
novelist, Deek, not a talker. The movies are for talkers.

New York is what it always is: fast, funny, moving,
sad. Millionaires stepping over winos. Skyscrapers going
up next to churches. Speed and filth, excess and starva-
tion. Noise beyond noise. People, business, and consumption, consumption, consumption. Books, magazines,
food, clothes, news—especially news, from the trivial to
the profound. I consume, therefore I am. That's the motto
of this city. But unlike LA, the diet here is information. It's
suckled morning, noon, and night. On the streets, in the
subways, and high up in the steel towers that float in the
microwaves like antennae in a sea of addiction. People
read everywhere—in cabs, in restaurants, on subways,
even walking down the street. But don't get any romantic
notions of literacy. It's crap they immerse themselves in—
the *Post* or whatever paperback *Time* magazine says they
should all be digesting this week. I'm sure to them it's a
way of seeming informed. To an outsider it appears to be
a mechanism for avoiding the so-called eye to eye the city
is famous for. It's the city of the modern soul, Deek—
everything is of human design and origin. The only thing

17

left is to construct a dome over it so that light and air can also be manufactured.

So why am I so happy? I don't know. Maybe I was born for perverse artificiality. It does challenge you to be God—if I make everything, then I alone am responsible. That, my friend, is the pressure, the so-called edge you feel here. It prods one, as it were, to produce.

Funny, huh, Deek? Your friend JJ finding God in New York City? I'll tell you something, that's not all I've found. But I'll save that for next time. . .

Keep writing. I love the whole idea of conducting my life through letters for a while.

Your future neighbor by the sea,
JJ

DOWN BY THE RIVER

Wed., January 18

J. J. Towne
c/o Futterman
183 Central Park West
New York, NY 10023

JJ—

I wanted you to know that I've gotten the messages. It isn't that I don't want to talk to you. It's that I do. But I can't. Ask Dot. She'll explain.

Sorry.
Andee

Miss Andee O'Neill
c/o "Down by the River"
Warwick Studios
5460 Seventh Ave.
New York, NY 10020

Andee—

Thanks for the note. I guess it was dumb of me to try you at home. I talked to Dot and she filled me in about Matt. So, am I taking my life in my hands to write you too?

  I don't care. I want to see you. How about lunch tomorrow? I'll be at Lenge on Columbus Ave. 12:45. There's a small room in back where no one will see us. I know the show only breaks for 45 minutes. I'll take it.

See you there.
JJ

It is midnight and I've just prayed to a starry California night sky for strength. I couldn't get myself to eat today. Just the thought of food made me sick. Rudi knows something is wrong. It's amazing how animals pick up on emotion. Deek told me the other day that they can hear the human heart beating and they sit right up with any rise in pulse. I'm not sure I believe that. Imagine what the world would sound like if your hearing was that sensitive. Not unlike the way everything sounds to me today— poised to assault, on the verge of overwhelming, like a wave of your worst fears all allied in a sickening wall of noise. California is no place for the self-conscious. How did I end up in this house afraid and alone? I look out at the canyon at my doorstep, whether by day or night, and I think, that's what I have inside me, that open space emptiness. This is a secret I share only with a dog. My husband is on the other side of the world. All at once, life has dropped a continent between us. And the sound of my own voice trying to bridge the gap disgusts me.

Thursday, January 19

Mr. J. J. Towne
c/o Futterman
183 Central Park West
New York, NY 10023

Dear JJ,

How are you, my love? I've been thinking of you all day, imagining your sweet amber eyes poised over your beautiful tiny handwriting. What's happening? I keep trying to picture you in your paisley den writing at an unfamiliar table (did you say it was round?) until they shut the lights on the Empire State Building down. Is New York being good to you? Is Futterman?

I was glad to hear about Dot Penner coming in on the situation. It seems to me that it offers a balance somehow and maybe leaves you less at the mercy of one person's taste or demands. Especially since you find it easier to talk to her than to the others. Funny too—I asked around at the studio and more people seem to know her name than Futterman's. I suppose that's because of the soap, but who are we to argue with visibility, right? Some Hollywood sage once said that the only bad publicity is no publicity at all. I know the play will be yours no matter what, so I say let the rest fall where it may. The more people you have behind you, the better the play's chances.

Rudi and I are okay, if a little bit lonesome. We were just out back doing our Starlight, Starbright for tonight and you should be lucky enough to have what we wished come true. I'm about to get in bed and read myself to sleep. I have six scripts to suffer through this weekend and judging from the titles it doesn't look to be even cheap thrills. But I'm not complaining. It beats writing music that no one ever hears. And David is terrific to work for even if he is pickier than I am. It's kind of nice being around someone who doesn't expect to be pleased. The only pressure is looking for the surprise that might make his day.

That's about it. Hope you're fine. No doubt you'll be hitting New York's finest over the weekend. Raise one to us. The canyon seems empty without you, and Rudi needs a good run. I may take her to the beach to see Deek tomorrow. We could both use some human contact.

Love you, always,
Lynn

Miss Andee O'Neill
c/o "Down by the River"
Warwick Studios
5460 Seventh Ave.
New York, NY 10020

Andee—

Do you know the Peter Handke play, *The Ride Across Lake Constance*? The title comes from an old European folk tale about a traveler who walked one step at a time through a night blizzard and realized that he had crossed the treacherous frozen lake only when he arrived on the other side and someone there told him.

That's what it was like yesterday when you told me everything about you and Matt. But we're already there on the other side, aren't we?

And I feel so alive. I don't know what to say. I guess I'd forgotten this sensation and done something I never thought I'd do—assumed that living and forgetting were one and the same thing. But they're not, are they? I don't ever want to forget again. I don't think I'll be able to. Not after the feel of that kiss.

Please call me. Or messenger over a note like last time. It isn't even 24 hours since we sat in that restaurant but already I can't stand it.

JJ

Mr. Richard Case
27 Saltair Road
Malibu, CA 90233

Dear Deek,

I've been walking in circles all day—from the Dakota
down Central Park West to 59th and then up Columbus
Ave. to 72nd and back over to the Dakota—and I just
don't know what to do. If I see one more baby boutique
or sidewalk café with lovers in the window licking ice
cream cones I'm going to puke. Did I tell you the Upper
West Side has turned into café society? There's a night-
hang by that very name. Who knows where the intellects
have gone? Back to the Village maybe . . . Anyway, I
gotta write you, buddy. Somebody else has to know.
   I think I'm in love.
   I was with Dot Penner and the Rabbit (that's Dot's
nickname for Sevi Paretti's brother, who she lives with)
last Saturday night at this place called Melon's on Amster-
dam and 76th, when who should come in but this girl
who is on Dot's soap with her. Now, I've never watched
the show, but the minute I see this girl I just about boil
over. I mean I was dead cold stunned. She's also a model
and I know you've seen her face staring at you in your
dreams the same as I have.
   So I try to be cool because she's with a guy (naturally), but she runs up to Dot (who is standing right next to
me) and gives her a big hug and while they're hugging,
her eyes lock onto mine. And I mean lock, my friend. I
don't think I've ever seen two women hug for that long in

25

a public place. She was hypnotized, as was I. And not at the sight of Dot—they're together every day.

So Dot knows, of course. She's felt the electricity through the embrace and she's aware that I'm the one who's standing behind her. She sees this happen at least once a week with guys. But not with Andee. (That's her name—Andee O'Neill.) Understand? Well, Dot did. She told me later she'd never seen two people simultaneously turn that shade of red. Unfortunately she also said she feared for my life.

See, Andee lives with this guy she's come to the bar with and his idea of independence is letting her go to the bathroom by herself. Seems he plucked her off the streets of South Boston when she was a teenager (she's only 22 now) and got her started modeling. With her looks it wasn't long before she had a little career going, so naturally they became an item and she moved in with him. Well, word spread, as did her picture and résumé, and before long Matt Stanese (that's his name) decides it's time to try New York. So they come down here for a few days to look around, and inside of the first week they're in town Andee is offered a running part on *Down by the River* and the network puts her under a possessory contract. One week, pal! I'm telling you, the woman is outstanding.

So anyway, there I am with a couple of G&T's in me staring at Venus on the half shell who's also staring at me, when I see this big-knuckled hand reach toward me. I guess I didn't hear but Dot is introducing this guy Stanese to me and he's reaching out to shake. I take his hand and he moves me out of range of his lady and acts all smooth and happy to meet me. He's heard about Dot producing my play and he says he looks forward to seeing it, and before I know it he's buying me another drink and asking me all about myself. The guy is decent even if he is wearing a silk shirt open one too many buttons.

So I'm talking to him and Andee's talking to Dot and

I'm looking at Dot, who is looking at Andee looking at me and before I know it the Rabbit is taking me by the arm to the john. Well, I don't have to go but with the G&T's in me it doesn't seem like such a bad idea (besides the Rabbit goes to the bathroom about every twenty minutes to powder his nose and the powder is movie-time quality, if you get my drift), so I go. Inside, the Rabbit takes me into a stall, we both powder our tootskies a bit, and he smiles at me.

"Hands off," he says.

And not being sure whether he's talking about the toot or what, I lift my hands in mock surrender and smile.

"Stanese's a family man," the Rabbit goes on, "and he doesn't like his pride and joy going for rides with strangers." The Rabbit's seen the electric spark outside too.

"They're married?" I ask like a jerk.

"No," the Rabbit says, "I wasn't talking about that kind of family."

Right, my friend. Yours truly has fallen head over heels for a Mafia princess. Seems Stanese now represents his Boston family's interests on the isle of Manhattan, and he counts Andee O'Neill high on his list of priorities. You don't get a late night phone call or a note in the mail when he discovers you've been eyeing his lady. You get your dick handed to you for safekeeping by a guy with sandpaper hands.

"Capice?" The Rabbit smiles.

"Hey, Rabbit," I answer, "if you saw the look in my eyes, you had to see what was in hers."

"What was in hers is of no importance, JJ." He almost pleads with me.

"What do you mean?" I volley, half angry at the Rabbit's audacity and half-moved by his almost parental concern. "Isn't it the twentieth century here in New York too?"

"You don't understand," he mumbles while dropping

27

the stash in a sewn-in pocket in his Italian boxers, "guys like Stanese, they don't live in our world."

"Yeah, and I don't live in theirs," I shoot back, now feeling hyped from the toot.

"Right," the Rabbit answers. "Just see to it you remember that."

And then he's gone. And I'm standing looking at a toilet, imagining my face being held in swirling filthy waters by some goon out of a gangster film. "Bullshit," I bounce off the tiles that are contoured from decades of weighty New York heels contemplating the universe that always exists in a men's room stall. I stare at these faded white tiles, reading them the way a golfer reads a green before stepping up to the most important putt of his life. "Things like that don't happen. Not in real life," I mumble. And after looking at my own eyes in a mirror and seeing only resolve, I'm back out at Melon's heading right back to Andee O'Neill.

We make some small talk the rest of the evening within the group. Perfectly innocent. Everyone laughing and drinking. You get the picture. *Desire Under the Elms. The Homecoming.* Every smile is our smile. Every laugh our laugh. Everything anyone says is a code for the silent conversation jumping like a high-voltage arc between our eyes. And everyone knows but no one says. And somehow before the night is over I manage to slip her a note scribbled on a matchbook. (God, this sounds like a soap, doesn't it? Well, they say cliché always has its root in truth. . . .) And I see her read the note and look up slowly with about the sexiest slow rise of the eyes I have ever witnessed in my life, bar none, even in the movies. She's shy and knowing, innocent and experienced, in control and out, she wants me and she's afraid. Most of all, she's just staring. Then she tilts her head ever so slightly and shakes it side to side in tiny quick hints that it's up to me. And then Stanese's putting her in a great long coat right in

28

front of me. Silky black hair tucked inside a high collar. Tight black sweater just down to where the smallest waist you've ever seen dips into jeans I can practically taste. And then they're gone. Out into the cold night. And I'm left with the wilted lime and melted ice in the bottom of my last G&T.

"Don't," the Rabbit says to me as he and Dot get up to leave. But behind his back Dot smiles at me and nods. And I know there is a conversation we must have alone.

Which we do. And in which Dot tells me the same story that the Rabbit unloaded on me in the john, but with one important exception. Seems Andee is grateful for all that Stanese has done for her, but there's also some Pygmalion stuff mixed in here that's starting to work against him (i.e., she's feeling her oats now that she's in Fat City and is becoming less and less comfortable with Don Corleone as she's becoming more and more comfortable with herself).

"She thinks you're adorable." Dot smiles. "She told me she couldn't stop looking at your mouth when you talked."

"She thinks *I'm* adorable . . ." I squeak, trying to hide the fact that I practically just came in my pants. "How do I get to her?"

"That's your problem," Dot says with a wry squint of her baby blues.

And it is. Even as I speak. But suffice it to say that I managed to have lunch with her yesterday in this Japanese hang, and after we both watched sashimi slide down each other's throats in some Japanese perversion of the Tom Jones table scene, I was the recipient of a sweet kiss the likes of which I don't remember even imagining in my direst fantasies. I'm telling you, Deek, I'm in love. She even knows I'm married. ("That's cake compared to what I have to deal with," she says to me.)

So what do I do? I'm walking around in circles

29

today, like I told you, thinking of her, thinking of me, of Lynnie, even of Rudi, for God's sake, of my entire existence. I had to say this to somebody. Forgive me if I sound like a school kid. That's the way I feel.

Help me, Deek. Either tell me this kind of thing really happens in people's lives or wake me up with a cold hard slap. I'm a friend in need, so do the deed. Soon.

JJ

P.S. She even plays tennis.

Funny how when you're separated from someone you love you seem to view every little thing you do in terms of them. JJ left almost three weeks ago now and I still think of him when I wash out a coffee mug or make the bed or feed Rudi or drive down the hill to the market. When he's here, I wish I could have the house to myself so that I wouldn't have a witness to every little thing I do. Now that he's gone, I feel that I need him as a frame of reference. What will I do if I'm right and he doesn't come back? What will it take to develop a new frame of reference? My work certainly isn't enough. I can write script reports in my sleep. My music maybe . . . ? I'm going out to the beach this afternoon to visit Deek. It'll be interesting to see if I take JJ's route or the route that causes us to quarrel, the one I supposedly prefer.

Sunday, January 22

Mr. J. J. Towne
c/o Futterman
183 Central Park West
New York, NY 10023

Dear JJ,

I'm home now and I decided to write because I couldn't stop thinking about our call all the way back in the car. I thought you'd be happy to hear from Deek and me at the same time. Even Rudi got excited when we told her she could say hi to her old man. But you sounded so funny, so down. Maybe just a bad Sunday there this time? I hope it isn't something with the play that you didn't want to talk about with Deek on the line. Is everything okay? You know, if you're having trouble working there, just say the word and we'll be at the airport to bring you back where you belong. Or where it might be better for you. You know what I mean. I guess I'm reaching. But when you get all quiet like that, what else can I do? I just want to help.

Rudi and I had a great time with Deek. The beach was just what the doctor ordered. I think I was starting to get cabin fever here. You know me: you lock me up with my own mind and the result isn't always peaches and cream. I think it was obvious to Deek that we needed airing out. He couldn't get us in off the sand yesterday, even after the sun was long gone down. You should have seen Rudi—hair all matted and covered with sand, seaweed, gum wrappers, twigs, you name it. We had to give her a bath but we did take a picture for the scrapbook. I'll

32

save it for you. I hope you don't mind that we stayed over. Deek was so sweet about it. He's a good friend, JJ. He really cares about us.

Anyway, I have to do some work now and make up for the lost time. Not that David will give a shit. The only thing he gets upset about is when I'm not padding the expense account enough. It's the studio, he says. They think if you're not using their money outrageously, then you can't be doing your job.

Hope you're all right, my love. I'll let you tell me what's going on when you're ready.

L&K,
Lynn

It started out innocently enough. There we were on the beach and the sun was hissing into the ocean, a huge red fireball, setting everyone and everything aglow like prisms. Sensation set loose by light, angle, point of view. We were just trying to towel the sand out of Rudi's coat, when his eyes caught mine. We were bent over, laughing. And there was his face. And mine. Two friends' faces. Of the long-time variety. It passed. Or rather, we let it pass. I wrapped a towel around my shoulders but my nipples were so hard I thought they would push right through the nap. I felt them through my suit. Through the towel. Through his glance. He suggested a bath would be in order. For Rudi. I agreed.

We walked up to the house. Wooden deck. Sand on the feet. Air starting to turn cool. Goose flesh. Door sliding open. Shivers on the red tile inside. The dog flopping, panting, wagging her long feathered tail. Dropping sand across the floor. A flash from his camera. Pictures of Rudi. Of us. White teeth on sunburned faces. Two beers from the kitchen. The cush of the tops opening. The foam on his upper lip. His throat as he swallows.

Then the big bathroom. Sunken tub overlooking the Pacific. The sun is in the ocean but you can still see it. Like a hot coal expanding in waves as it sends out its last glimmers of light. We drop our towels as he turns on the water. I pick up Rudi and one of her paws scratches my stomach. He touches the scratch as a trace of blood appears. And then she's in the bubbling water. Smiling

34

her dog smile as he runs his fingers through her coat. Long smooth strokes along the line of her back. Then short tickling ones beneath her, on her tummy, under the water. She's in ecstasy at the touch of his fingers. And then he squeezes the shampoo on and works it into a lather. Some of it splashes into his eye and instinctively I reach out to wash it away. I cup some water and raise it to his cheek. Several times. And he smiles. So do I.

And then we're in the water. With the dog. Rubbing her and giving her the time of her life. Washing and rinsing. Rinsing and washing. And finally she is clean. Her coat actually squeaks. He opens the drain. And we let her shake off. And that is a mistake. Or not. Depending on your point of view. The angle. The prism has been moved in here. In this bathroom. With us.

We are covered with splatter. We look at ourselves and laugh. He picks up a towel as Rudi runs to a rug to roll around on her back. He wipes out the tub, then turns the water on again. This time full force. Several spouts at once. All of them shooting a stream of steaming water toward the center of the huge tub. And he reaches for some mineral bath and pours it into the rising water and it foams around our ankles and tickles as it starts a slow rise up our legs. And then he is handing me my beer. And we're both swallowing hard and smiling with our eyes. And I don't know what makes me do it but I step forward and pour some of mine over his shoulders. Sunburnt shoulders. And the white beer foam drops down across his chest, washing across one of his nipples before it falls the straight vertical line on his stomach to the waistband of his bathing suit, which, smiling, he removes. And I am not shocked. I am smiling too. He is a beautiful man and all this time, all these years, I have always known it. I untie my own suit. I pour the rest of my beer across my breasts. And he is kissing them, sucking malt from between them. And we are in the water. It is swirling

35

around our necks. His hands are on me, inside me. Mine are on him, around him. And our mouths become one, lips one, shoulders one, chests one, sunburnt stomachs under swirling waters one, and I am looking at him and he is looking at me, and our two heads are dancing on the surface of the water as tiny lifeboats on a sea, and I am gone, sinking, like the sun outside, to another world, where heat is dancing on the ocean floor as above the night shivers, and we have become divers, our bed the waves which wash over us, around us, between us, inside us, until the heat is gone.

Then sleep. The white bed. The dog between us. Sound of the sea outside. Peace on earth. For a night my husband is dead. Instead of me.

But then JJ's voice again. The next day. Cross-country small talk. Silence. Does he know something? What? Deek says I am imagining things. And it is true. I am. Like what life would be like filled with days like that one. What I would be like filled with thoughts like these. What his touch will be like. The next time I accept it. How I will find words to explain all of this. To me.

Wednesday, January 25

Mr. J. J. Towne
c/o Futterman
183 Central Park West
New York, NY 10023

Dear JJ,

I got your letter yesterday and I've really been at a loss for how to respond. Don't get me wrong—it isn't shock or anything as simple as that. I guess I'm just surprised, and as a friend of both yours and Lynn's, I've been looking for the right words.

First of all, you know that I would never slap anything like this down. You're talking to a man who cherishes sin in a way he likes to think of as original. (And from what I know so far, this situation is definitely original. . .)

But second, and perhaps most important, is the urgency I sense from you. And at this I'm almost ready to suggest that we give thanks with prayer.

JJ, my friend, I haven't heard anything like this come out of you in years. I don't need to remind you of what you said to me down at the pier just before you left, do I? You practically went to your knees to ask that something happen in your life to reignite your senses, to remind you that there might be something to get up for in the morning, to give you reason to live. As you'll recall, I suggested that you could think of this opportunity with the play as just such a spark, but you obviously didn't agree. It haunted me for days the way you answered, "Yeah, I guess I could . . ." with that scary flat intonation you get in your voice when you're down. But I understood. You've been through too many ups and downs with your plays and with all the hopes and expectations everyone, including you, has had for them over the years. I felt a bit like that myself at the time, to be honest. I mean, about my movie. You're like me, JJ. The pleasure you get from your writing happens mostly at your desk. What comes after that is more a reason to fall into sleep than to rise and shine.

Speaking of which, dig the latest from George Davis. The studio has changed its mind on the film again. They not only don't want my boy catching sight of himself in a mirror during sex; they don't want him catching sight of himself at all. Not even in a store window. Seems they now think he'd be better off "not consummating the relationship," (their words) and keeping his dreams intact. Better to keep his desire for this girl in the realm of fantasy, they say, where it can't be diminished by the reality of flesh.

Fairly sophisticated concept for some studio V.P.'s, wouldn't you say? Except that it turns my character into that kind of alienated loner that I have absolutely no interest in. The whole point of the story was to see what happens to a guy who jumps in without analyzing the consequences of his actions ahead of time. Which is, I guess, what I'm also telling you to do, my friend. It seems to me we're all capable of leaving our dreams be dreams. It's the rare person who can do something to make them into reality.

So while I certainly wouldn't like to think of you walking around New York City with a price on your head, I can't help but encourage you to pursue this thing with Andee. If it's nothing more than a good time and your energy being in one of its notorious upswings, then so be it. You'll at least leave the horrors of the last year behind you. If it's more than that, look what you might have to look forward to—namely, what you've been asking for, your reason to live.

In the meantime, know that Lynn is fine. I enjoyed having her out over the weekend and I promise to look after her for the time being if you like. Even Rudi needed to get out of that cliff dwelling you guys live in. Lucky dog came out of it with a bath I doubt any of us will soon forget.

You're really very lucky, you know, JJ. Lynn weathers these trips of yours with great style. Seems to me you're in the enviable position of having your cake and eating it too.

Keep me posted on your appetite.

As always,
Deek

DOWN BY THE RIVER

Wednesday, January 25

Mr. J. J. Towne
c/o Futterman
183 Central Park West
New York, NY 10023

JJ—

I got your note here at the studio Monday morning and I
have to tell you, I knew it would be here when I arrived.
Still, when I walked in and saw it in my mail drawer, my
heart kind of jumped. I like what you said about *The Ride
Across Lake Constance*. The problem for me is I'm still out
there and now I know it's ice beneath me. I feel like I'm
walking around waiting for every step to be my last.

Still, I couldn't get you out of my mind all weekend.
You have the sweetest mouth I've ever seen on a man and
I could taste your kiss anytime I closed my eyes and
thought about it. I guess I was doing that a little more than
I realized too. Maybe more than I should. Matt asked me
once what I was dreaming about. And you know what I
said like an idiot? California. Not the brightest thing I
could have come up with, but I guess you've got me
thinking. Trouble is, now Matt is probably going to come
home with tickets to fly out there. You have to be careful
what you say around him. Give him an idea and he's
dangerous.

I don't know what I'm going to do. I still care for
him. It's just I'm not the same little girl I was when I first

met him. He means well and he's certainly done a lot for me, but I can tell you, I felt more in your one kiss than I've felt in the three years I've been with him. I've been waiting for my moment, JJ. And for someone like you. Is this it? Are you the one? How do I do this? How do we?

I've got the questions, huh? Are you the answer? I swore I wouldn't even write this note to you. It's unfair to ask so much. But as you can see, I made it only two days before I couldn't stop myself. And that's what I feel like, JJ. I can't stop. I want you. Or I at least want to find out if I want you. And if you want me. That's not too much to ask at this point in my life, is it?

I'll try to call you at lunchtime tomorrow. I think Matt may be going up to Boston on Friday, so maybe we can work out something for the afternoon. I've already asked if they can do my scenes here in the morning. And Dot sometimes lends me her key. . .

I'm thinking of you.
Andee

Thursday, January 26

Miss Andee O'Neill
c/o "Down by the River"
Warwick Studios
5460 Seventh Ave.
New York, NY 10020

Andee—

Your voice in my ear is magic. I adore the sound. I know I won't sleep a bit tonight. I'll be staring at the clock until the sun comes up and it's tomorrow. I'll take a separate cab to Dot's, like you said. 2:15. I can't even breathe.

JJ

It's Friday already and I still feel like I'm waiting for the week to begin. I've been anxious, uneasy, since Monday. Kept putting things off. Didn't answer my phone or return calls that were on the machine. Never made it into the office. When I step outside, even to walk Rudi, I get out of breath. And it isn't smog. The air has been clear and flowing with winter sea currents. It's me. I'm afraid. And afraid of being afraid. Deek called again this morning. I've replayed the tape a dozen times. "Come out again tomorrow," he says. Is that what I'm afraid of? Come out again, Lynn Towne . . . Lynn Rodnick Towne. . . We know you're in there. The years haven't taken you away. Even if you've convinced yourself at times that they have. There's still someone to reckon with in there. Someone who's been disappointed by life even though she's had much of what she asked for. Where did your music go? And the feel of long silky hair on your naked back in the middle of the afternoon? And your penchant for poetry, meaningless though it may be to all around you? The hunger? The feel? The touch that they used to say you had? Deek said it. Last weekend at the beach. Where you communed with the sea once again. Where the moontide pulled at your heart and washed crust from your eyes. You opened your eyes. Beneath the water. So did he. You were cleansed, reborn, if just for a moment. When was the last time you could say you shared such a moment with another human being?

I will call him. Right now. But "Watch out," David Byrne keeps screaming from my radio, "you might get what you're after. . . Burning Down the House!"

Lynn—

I've just hung up the phone with you and I'm going to write you this note and hand it to you the minute you get here tomorrow, if you get here.

I'm glad you told me the things you did. I've been experiencing much of the same anxiety all week. How could we avoid it, given the circumstances? I've known you for nine years. As my best friend's wife. As one of my best friends. But now all is changed. I've made love to you. I know you in a way I never did before. Or do I? It's funny, but it didn't seem like the first time to me somehow, even though it was. I guess I've always felt that close to you. Still, it's different.

Now you ask me what are we going to do about it? And I answer maybe everything, maybe nothing. I'm not being flip. I'm trying to be what I've always been with both you and JJ: straight. You're the only people on earth I've never lied to and even though you and I have a secret at the moment, it doesn't make what we say to JJ and what we say to each other untrue. What I saw in your eyes, what you saw in mine, was honest and real. I touched your heart, not your body. And you touched mine. What we do about that is try to accept it as the gift it was to both of us when it happened. I don't know if it will ever happen again. If not, I will accept that. If so, I will try, with you, to understand it. What I don't want to do is cheapen it with guilt, make it less than what it was, what it is. I have the rest of the world to try to do that to my experience. Let's leave this above the thorns if we can, where fragrance carries us by our senses to what we long for: the invisible, the heartfelt, the true.

If after reading this you can look at me and smile, then I'll know what I already know, that we didn't do something *to* one another or *to* ourselves, but rather that something happened between us, that we shared it, savored it, caressed it as in a dream and then awoke all the better for it in the morning.

I'll be waiting, watching, to see.

Love,
Deek

45

Saturday, January 28

Mr. Richard Case
27 Saltair Road
Malibu, CA 90233

Dear Deek,

Last week I was drifting, walking in circles, and this week
I'm flying, walking on air. You said you wanted me to
keep you informed, so . . .

I made love to her yesterday, Deek. The old man had
to go up to Boston to break some legs or something (just
kidding [I hope]) and Andee managed to get the afternoon
off from the show. Dot Penner, who is rapidly becoming
friend as well as associate, gave us the key to her apartment and the rest, shall we say . . .

Needless to say, we fucked our brains out. The girl
is 22, pal. Raised on head. If my teen icon was Mick
Jagger's hair, hers was his lips. She loves mouths, and the
minute ours touched again, the room boiled over. I have
never—except maybe the first time I slept with Lynnie all
those years ago—felt anything like it. She's hard, lithe,
and dark, Deek. Very different from Lynnie. And I'm not
just talking bodies (though I'm sure you'd have no objec-
tion if I were). I'm in a world I've never known before
(though not for lack of interest), and now I'm not sure I'll
ever get back out.

We spent the entire afternoon inside each other. I
kept looking further into her eyes and, funny enough,
what I saw was all virgin territory. She's no stranger to
sex, but I think she is to love. Her relationship with
Stanese was the first of her adult life and to say it's been

46

one of convenience doesn't do it justice. She cried at one point when she tried to tell me it's been like sleeping with her father at times. (I guess her real father tried some of that on her, too, so it was no easy admission.) I know one can be prone to exaggeration in these moments, but I think it might have been the first time she let herself go out of true desire. If I'm wrong, then I'm not sure I'd want to be there when she hit true—I don't know if I'd survive it.

So we stayed on the burner until meltdown and then we solidified as best we could. But I'll tell you, it was like we were melted wax figures and even though they poured us back into our original moulds, the cooled-out figurines were but facsimiles of our former selves. I stumbled back here to Futterman's and she grabbed a cab down to SoHo. I had no dinner—or should I say no hunger—and my dreams last night were, for the first time since I got here, nonexistent. How could I dream anything after a day like that?

This morning, looking at myself in the mirror, my only thought is that I hope her youth will have put her back together faster than my experience seems to be working for me. Otherwise when Stanese rolls in we might both be on our way to the East River.

So now what, pal? Go with it, be bad, you told me, which I did, like your hero, and now I feel done, for good. See, unlike you seemed to be suggesting in your letter, this thing is no result of excess energy, like some fling in the night. This *is* energy. Pure and lasting. I'm feeling renewed, I'm feeling optimistic, I'm feeling like myself as I would like myself to be.

But where do I go from here? I've been looking at Lynnie's picture all morning, wondering how I can be feeling all I am when the two of us were born to be together, when we have been together for twelve years, since we were babies, schoolkids, kids the age of Andee

47

O'Neill. Can a marriage dissolve over passion, Deek? over a renewal of lust? In some ways, the education of marriage seems to me to be an active distrust of the physical. Its pleasures last about two minutes. Or in memory until the next two minutes come along. Is that what is happening to me? Am I locked into the hypo time of sex where what now feels to me like eternal pleasure will later be revealed as a split-second on the continuum of inevitable disappointment? Please say no. Or yes. Or what you always say, which is whatever you want. I'll be on my way to finding out more next week—it looks like Andee may have a few days off from the show. . .

Always,
JJ

Saturday night, January 28

Lynn Towne
8541 Coldwater Canyon
Los Angeles, CA 90056

Lynnie—

I'm alone here tonight with the city out my window and I
feel like talking to you. I called but got the machine, so I
guess I'll resort to what I seem to be these days, a letter
writer. It's not so bad though. I think, in fact, it may still
be the best way to talk from the heart without all the
intrusions of speech. This way all you're dealing with is
the inadequacy of language.

Anyway, wherever you are tonight, I hope you're
enjoying yourself. I said hi to Rudi on the tape just in case
you left the volume up on the machine, and now I'm
feeling guilty about it. I mean, what does a dog think if
she's lying there in an empty house at night and out of
thin air suddenly hears her master's voice professing love
and longing? I don't know if it's ever been established that
dogs dream but I bet I know one who thinks she does
tonight.

It's funny to think of the house from here. When
you're in this city you really do believe the world ends at
the Hudson River. I look out at all the lights some nights,
all the lives, flickering like stars, each one laying claim to
being the center of the universe, oblivious to its neighbor,
and yet forming a pattern like the constellations in the
great whole of the night, and no matter how hard I try, all
I can ever come up with is a sound almost like a sigh that

49

whispers, "New York . . ." Maybe someday I'll write about this time I'm spending here. It feels like the stuff of something—what I can't say just yet.

The play is coming along. I've been whipping through Act I, at times almost unable to stop the flow of the changes I'm making. It *is* different, but then so am I. I always wonder about that, how lines can be perfect one day and inadequate the next. But I guess it has to do with the nature of the theater itself as a living form. Just as people change from day to day, so perhaps do characters. Until they're frozen in time by performance, by human voices throwing words out into the abyss where, once spoken, nothing can ever truly be held on to or taken back. It's the thing I love and hate about writing plays. They exist really only as light and sound, both of which by definition must remain in motion. And for those who chase motion, there can be no rest.

Don't mean to get philosophical on you. I guess that's what happens when you're left with an enormous Central Park West apartment to yourself on a Saturday night and you're not quite sure what you're doing in it. Futterman and his wife are in black tie tonight for a live concert he's produced for PBS. I watched the first few minutes but he had some guy introducing "tonight's works of the ages" like Leonard Pinth-Garnell on that *Saturday Night Live* bit, Great Moments in Bad Theater. For the first time since I've been here, I paused in true doubt. (Actually the second. The paisley wallpaper was the first. . . .) After all, his reputation *is* mostly in television. Oh well, I have to proceed on faith, I guess. Maybe he was just giving them what they wanted, doing what was necessary to get the show on. I certainly hope so. . .

And he *is* being good to me. Along with everyone else. Maggie calls me every afternoon to cheer me on and then Futterman comes home to take me out to dinner at yet another new restaurant up here on the west side. (It's unbelievable how many there are. Columbus Avenue is the yellow brick road for all the Yupsters. It's getting almost like Ventura Boulevard in the Valley, where something pops up while you sleep at night.)

And Lady Di (as in Aimsley) had Maggie and me down to her apartment for a couple of beers. She lives off Union Square and plays her tough-guy image to the hilt. It's an old industrial building—and not the kind that has been made into a bunch of chic lofts either. It's linoleum and fluorescent lights and winos in the hallways. Her bathroom betrays her though. Fluffy pink long-haired throw rugs and a shelf filled with every Opium product Saint Laurent makes. I got homesick at the smell. I don't care if we end up on welfare someday—I want you to promise me you'll always find a way to wear some of that stuff.

So, that's about it for now, I guess. Futterman's daughter just came in, so I'll cut this off. Have I told you about her? She works for him and lives over on the east side, and get this, she's a twin. Don't get too excited though—even if it is still one of your husband's all-time fantasies, I'm afraid the Futterman girls will not be the ones. Not that this one would mind. She's always showing up when I'm alone or showering or taking off my shirt, but she's harmless. I kind of like her and she always has some great smoke on her. In fact, I think she's one of the few people I've ever known who is addicted to it. She got offered a production job on a TV show that spends part of the year in other countries and she actually turned it down because she couldn't see herself going through customs with dope on her person and she couldn't see her person existing without dope. Ah, the problems of the rich . . .

Take care, my love. I've been thinking about you a lot lately. When I tell people I've been married for twelve years, they look at me like I must be one of

51

the chosen few. And I have to admit, I still like the idea of that.

Talk to you soon.

Love,
JJ

Sunday, January 29

Andee, my love,

Surprise! We leave tonight. First class! I'm so glad you thought of it. Three days alone with you in California— we'll feel like we've died and gone to heaven. Wait till you see what I've arranged for us when we get there too. Pack your swimsuits, especially that little red one that you look good enough to eat in. I adore you, my love.

xx,
Matt

Mr. J. J. Towne
c/o Futterman
183 Central Park West
New York, NY 10023

JJ—

What did I tell you? Sorry . . .

I think I love you.
Andee

54

Sunday night, January 29

A second weekend with Deek. And the result? I'm filled
with memories of when I first met JJ. And they're sense
memories, not a conscious calling up of events for com-
parison or anything as small as that. It's as though the
mystery of crawling into someone's sexuality, into their
insides, triggers a navigating mechanism in the brain which
leads one blind through the darkness and back to a certain
knowledge, a certain recollection, an instinct. Yes, I've
been here, I know this groping, here I must run ahead,
here lag behind, here look into his eyes, here be shy, stay
within mine. . . . It *is* a dance in darkness. And the human
soul is enlarged by a clever step improvised in the night.

When I first met JJ he was working in the Centicore
Bookshop back in Ann Arbor. He was thin and blond and
had the kindest amber eyes I had ever looked into. We
had both graduated from Michigan and found ourselves
unable to leave town. It was the end of the 60's, which is
to say it was the 70's, and he wanted to be a writer and I
a musician. He had won a Hopwood Prize for the first
play he ever wrote and I was the only woman in my class
at the music school to earn a degree in theory and composition. Upon graduation he found himself selling books.
I was playing in a rock and roll band.

I went into Centicore often (they had the best poetry
section in town) and we usually smiled at each other
without speaking. But one night (JJ worked the four-to-
midnight shift to leave his days free for writing) as I was
leafing through a book of poems by Mark Strand, he just
came up behind me and said, "Incredible, right?" Then

55

he turned the book's pages, though it was still in my hands, to show me what he said was his favorite line in all of modern poetry. I remember the sight of his delicate finger pointing on the page to what I knew even at that moment was our future together. The line read, "There are stones in the sea no one has seen."

I don't know if it was that night that I took him home with me for good (we both change our minds about that), but if not, it was soon. In my memory we fall from the page of that book onto my bed beneath a very 60's Chinese lantern to make the most perfect love I have, to this day, ever experienced. Our very skin seemed to belong together, as did our smells, our voices, our tastes. I had kept a journal as a young girl in which I prayed to the sky for Him, and the moment JJ touched me I knew He had arrived. We were two baby blondies who had opened our eyes at the same instant only to see each other against the colorful panorama that was that time in the world. In the instant he entered me we became one, never to be parted, and we passed into a state of grace never to be equaled, never to be surpassed.

I thought of all this as I fell asleep last night at Deek's. As the ocean crashed on the beach, it seemed to carry on every wave a music long dead but not forgotten. In the band I played in back then, a guy named John Nemo used to do a song called "Lonesome Cities" that always broke my heart. I've heard what became of him on and off over the years but last night he was singing again. And JJ and I were back in that bed on East William Street in Ann Arbor. Our skin was warm, we had the perfect fit of spoons in a drawer, and the smell of vanilla was in the air. And I looked forward to the sun coming up in the morning.

Such is the nature of sex. We enter not into someone else, but into ourselves. And then we remember.

I remember you, JJ. I was in the arms of another last night. In another time. Another place. It was a dream. But still I was with you.

Sunday night, January 29, 1:30 AM,
somewhere over America

Mr. J. J. Towne
c/o Futterman
183 Central Park West
New York, NY 10023

Dear JJ,

I'm sitting here on the plane looking down at cities far
below and suddenly I feel like I have no past. After Friday
there is only the future. With you.

Maybe I thought I knew things. Maybe I thought I
had been experiencing things. Now I know nothing could
be further from the truth. I've never felt anything like that
in my life. I tried to tell you, but I couldn't find the words.
I still can't. I'll have to leave that to the writer. All I know
is you're on my mind and your touch is on my body. Still!
I'm sitting here at 30,000 feet with Matt at my side (asleep)
but my spirit is down there on the ground. With you.

I don't know how we're going to fix everything so we
can be together, JJ, but I have to have you. I want you to
know everything about me. I want to know everything
about you. I want to be your love. I want you to be mine.
I want to make love to you until it hurts. Until everything
in the world is fine. I want to give you the new start
you're looking for. And have you give me mine. I want
you, I want you, I WANT YOU!

Have to go. I can't have Matt see this and he's
waking up. I'll try to call if I can.

God, I do love you. Just this morning I was afraid to say it. Now I shout it to all the stars in the sky. I'm in love with JJ Towne! He's going to be mine!

Andee

Monday, January 30

Mr. J. J. Towne
c/o Futterman
183 Central Park West
New York, NY 10023

Dear JJ,

After much thought I've decided to say congratulations. And not just because you're balling the 22-year-old of all our dreams—I'll do my best to remain above that—but rather because I think you're being brave to follow your desire into such a landscape of danger. And here I refer not just to the specter of broken legs . . .

I guess I have to agree with what you say about marriage and the physical. It's just that it's hard for me to imagine the pleasure of sex with Lynn lasting only two minutes. If this is so with a woman of her intelligence and beauty, then no further testimony is needed—marriage should be outlawed immediately.

I think you're aware, though, that what you're really talking about is the nature of experience itself and the way it wreaks havoc on our enthusiasm. You sing this song, in fact, at the end of your letter, where you beg me to spare you from your own knowledge of disappointment. Sorry, pal, I can do a lot for you, but even if you were a character in the novel I'm writing, (which I have to tell you you are at this point), that would not be within my powers.

Which is not to say that it might not be within Andee's. In another part of your letter you say, ". . . this thing is no result of excess energy, like some fling in the night. This *is*

59

energy. Pure and lasting. I'm feeling renewed, I'm feeling optimistic, I'm feeling like myself as I would like myself to be." That, my friend, sounds like love, not sex, and I will not be put in the position of trying to draw boundaries where matters of love are concerned. Love is one of Nature's invisible forces, like gravity or the wind, and I would no sooner try to hold it in a cage than I would try to hold a candle to the night.

For myself, I have been known to fall in love with characters in my own stories and books to the point where I betray other characters in the same invention with something approaching joy. And this joy then carries over into the rest of my life until I begin noticing that I'm treating real people with more compassion and interest, and then they, in turn, are telling me that I seem happier and more alive. If this fictitious love, or love of fiction, if you prefer, can do all this, then imagine what the real thing might be capable of.

But here is where I seem to turn to you. Though I try to write about these pageants of the heart, you're the one who goes out into the world and acts them out, aren't you? You *are* like the guy in my movie—at least the way I originally wrote him—you *can* just jump in without analyzing all the consequences. Maybe that's why we stay such good friends. You need to do these things so you can live. I need to know such things are possible so I can write.

So you see, JJ, I have a great deal at stake in your adventures too. If this affair with Andee turns out to be the fresh start on life that I think you're hoping for, then I stand to gain from it as well. Your new energy, your ability to transform yourself, gives me new energy, inspires transformation in me. And like you looking forward to the next day, I can then look forward to the next page. After all, who knows what waits there? If surprises in art can become surprises in life, then the reverse must also be possible, right?

I assume the play is coming along as well. I wish you luck, and in so doing, I happily wish myself the same thing.

This is goddamn fun.

Best,
Deek

Dear Andee,

What are you to have done this to me? A drug that, once tasted, means certain addiction? All my senses are heightened. I'm seeing, hearing, smelling, and tasting things as though I'm a bear come from a cave at the first sign of spring. And my fingers, now that they have touched your skin, are tingling. I touch myself and they become you, your fingers, dancing on me, dancing that afternoon slow hand we danced into a scream. I think of you out there in that desert. Near my home. Sounds of unfamiliar birds in your ears. Unfamiliar smells on the wind. And I wish I were there to be your guide. To lead you through the night. Holding you. Tight. Listening to your smooth dark voice. You're talking to me, aren't you? I hear you. And I answer. You said the word love in this note I have here before me. Love, you said, you think. And I think too. That love is something that for a long time I have been proud to hold on to in memory or else have looked forward to with a kind of desperate longing but rarely have been able to point to, let alone feel, in the present.

I want you, Andee. It gives me chills to say it. But I want you. When I see you again I will watch as you read this. And as my words enter you like nightbirds and fly their way to your heart. And as your eyes come off the page to mine. To give me that look that we both knew would stop time. And sleep. And lives. We'll find a way, Andee. Okay? And it'll be so right that no one will even ask how or when or why.

I'm yours. Now.
JJ

Monday, January 30

Mr. J. J. Towne
c/o Futterman
183 Central Park West
New York, NY 10023

Dear JJ,

Well, here I am, probably minutes from your house but God knows how far from you. Matt is downstairs doing business with somebody, so I thought I'd sneak you another letter. I don't know, maybe I'd like to get caught, maybe that's why I'm taking the risk of putting things in writing. I don't care.

We got in in the middle of the night and I kept dozing off in the car on the way to the hotel. But the smells . . . You must have night-blooming jasmine all over this city. I kept waking up thinking I was in the country somewhere. It's funny, that's what it seems like here to me. They talk about the smog and everything, but it seems so fresh and clean. Very sexy. All I'd need is to be with you and I could imagine some things going on. . . .

This hotel is really a trip. Just like I've always heard. All pink and lush and filled with people dripping with money. I guess no matter how well you do, there's always going to be someone to make you feel like you're still on the wrong side of the tracks. For a girl from South Boston, though, I feel like I'm doing okay. Somebody recognized me in the Polo Lounge this morning and it really made Matt's day. He scraped one of his sunny-side up eggs onto a piece of toast and swallowed the whole thing in one gulp. I thought I was going to throw up but I signed the autograph instead.

Now I'm sitting here in a pretty yellow chair in our room and the sweetest breeze is blowing these white chiffon curtains across the back of my neck and I'm imagining it's you over my shoulder while I write. Oh, we could have some fun in this room, JJ. I'd lay you over there on that soft white bed and run my fingers over every square inch of your body. I'd kneel above you and let you try to come up through my hair to find my mouth the way you did at Dot's when we both kept laughing. I'd crawl under these flower sheets and make you come and find me and then I'd kiss you until you were dizzy and couldn't breathe. I'd make love to you until the jasmine outside bloomed and then get you dressed, feed you dinner, get you undressed, and start all over again.

I could imagine living here, JJ. You could write all day and we'd make love under the desert sky all night. Maybe they'd even let me in the movies. I keep hearing from people that if anybody could make the jump from daytime, it would be me. What do you think? Maybe your friend Deek could help me. Maybe I'll give him a call. Maybe I'll just stay here and make you come get me. What do you say, Mr. Playwright? If it's a choice between Broadway Dianne Aimsley and L.A. Andee O'Neill, where are the cards gonna fall? Huh? Just think before you answer though. And try to picture what I'm seeing right here in this pretty stucco room. . .

I'm going to go brush my hair. And I'm going to imagine my brush is your fingers. And then I'm going to go down to the tennis court and tell the pro he has to run a bunch of frustration out of me. And I'll ask him if he's ever hit with JJ Towne and if he's as good as he claims. And whether he answers yes or no, he'll get an argument from me. I'm going to argue with everybody today, JJ.

Because that's what I feel like doing. And maybe by sundown the world will surrender and leave us be what we want to be. You and me.

Love,
Andee

Mr. J. J. Towne
c/o Futterman
183 Central Park West
New York, NY 10023

Dear JJ,

It's about 7:30 and I just got home from the office to find your letter on the floor waiting to make me smile. It was lying right on top and Rudi was doing her jump-in-place dance as though she knew. Do you think that's possible? I know she smells you all over the paper when I open the envelope, so maybe she just smells right through it too. It was funny that you also wondered what she would think of your voice on the machine, because I was going to tell you what happened when I came home and played the message the other night. Her ears went up and she did one of her Jack Benny takes and then she whined for a good half hour. There is no doubt it played heavily on her mind.

So, you sound well. I'm glad the play is coming along. And I'm not surprised that you're making a lot of changes. I know you won't do anything to it that isn't for the better. It's like you said—until you actually get it in performance, you and it are going to keep changing. It's just strange how that guarantees fate a role in the creation, though. Even after all these years I guess I like to think of the process as a little more objective. Seems like when something is right it must be right, and therefore finished. No wonder all the writers like meetings with me, huh? I sometimes tell them their job is done.

Which reminds me—I saw a great piece of graffiti on the bulletin board in the commissary today. A writer says, "It works but let's make it better." The director says, "If it ain't broken, don't fix it." And the producer says, "It's perfect. Let's change it." We'll see if that applies when you finish, huh? The idea of Futterman as Leonard Pinth-Garnell makes me a little nervous too. But you say Maggie is right there on everything, so maybe she'll deflect any wandering from the path. And certainly Dot Penner and Dianne Aimsley are going to say what they like. I think it'll be all right, JJ. You've got enough variables in the situation to protect yourself. Just keep writing.

The Futtermans' daughter situation sounds promising too. You can't tell me you have your golden opportunity staring you right in the face and you're not going to do anything about it. How often do you think you're going to run into twins, one of whom smokes more dope than you do and likes to watch you undress? I say do it, my love. As long as you report the results with your normal sense of ironic detachment. (What a wife you have . . .)

Seriously, JJ, we agreed before you left that some of the trouble we've been having was because we've been just plain stale on each other. You don't spend 24 hours a day with someone for 12 years without some of that creeping in. So, if twins are what you want, then go ahead. Personally, I like the idea of one on one. I can't picture the logistics of two of everything coming at me. But if that's what you want, all power to you. Just don't bring home anything contagious. (I wonder if twins with herpes would have their viruses active at the same time. In the old days I'd have called up Herbie over at the ISR—I'm sure he could get a terrific grant to make a study of that one . . .)

Anyway, I'm hungry and Rudi's asking for a Milk-Bone and my fingers are tired from four script reports I did today, so I think I'll say good night, Gracie. I assure you we're still here even if your Mr. New-York-all-of-a-sudden eyesight tells you otherwise. (Maybe if the Hudson River weren't so foul-smelling and filthy, someone could get near enough to it to see across to the life on the other side.)

I also want to say that I like the idea of us communicating through letters right now too. I think it lets us reacquaint ourselves with a sense of each other's style. Kind of like the way you talked to me before I really knew you, when you were selective about what you let through (and vice versa). That's what style is, right? I think it's nice, to tell you the truth. Who knows—maybe we *are* among the chosen ones. And maybe it's because we allow things like this to happen over the course of our time together.

Take care of yourself, JJ. I'll always love you.
Lynn

This is great. My husband is playing with the idea of fucking twins on Central Park West, I'm fucking my husband's best friend, all of us are talking and writing letters back and forth, and I call it a sense of style. Well, maybe that's what it is. We used to say style was a lie, until the 80's, when it suddenly became fashionable again. But here we are. Our reflections in mirrors glare with our affectations. Our money spent ever so selectively flashes our good taste, goodwill, and most important, good credit. Even our faces are painted to reveal our so-called appreciation of "quality." But inside, the same hearts are beating. The same wounds are festering. The same idea of triumph over material desire looms as the great savior. But we have become liars, like all those before us. Because it was too hard to insist on the truth. And I am one of them. Even if I have my differences. The 70's were the time of the promiscuous "me" and during the 70's I was happily married. The 80's are the time of the return of the "happy young couple" and I am down at the beach sucking cock. Hail the rebel. Still on the wrong side of the line. Hail all you princes of the 80's—some of the great hypocrites of all time.

Tuesday, January 31

Mr. J. J. Towne
c/o Futterman
183 Central Park West
New York, NY 10023

Dear JJ,

I'm at the pool and I'm writing because I can't keep my mind off you in this heat. It's hard to believe it can be this nice out when it's freezing cold and snowing back there. What are you doing in New York in January, when it's like this out here? You must be dedicated or something.

Matt asked me before what I'm doing with the pen and paper all the time, so I'm afraid he's picking up on this. But I don't care. I showed him a page full of scratches and doodles and said I wasn't really writing anything. It keeps all the guys with the gold watches away, I said, which is true, and he bought it and went back inside. Fortunately he has one meeting after another lined up, so I get to be mostly by myself. And, in my thoughts, with you.

A woman recognized me before, of course, and it wasn't long before I was surrounded. A nice guy rescued me and then turned out to be a producer. He was gay, so there was nothing else going on, and I talked to him for about an hour. He said he watched my soap every day without fail but looked away when I asked him what he thought of me trying movies out here. I can't believe the way people always have to pigeonhole you. I mean, maybe the guy's nobody and it doesn't even matter, but right away he had to let me know I should stay in my place. Then when we're through talking, what do you think he asks me? If I'll sign a picture to Jeffrey, his lover. Give me a break.

I'll tell you, this hotel is really something though. You can sit looking out at the cars on Sunset and get sick. I mean, more Rolls-Royces went by while I was eating breakfast this morning than I've seen in my entire life. And I took a walk up behind the grounds on Crescent and the houses were like something out of your fantasies. I can't believe people actually live like this. You come around the curve, out of the trees that smell so good and are filled with the strangest birds, and there's this immaculate pink palace. It's like somebody remembered his dream from too good a night on the town and built it the next morning before he woke up and forgot.

I could get used to this, JJ. The people are friendly and nothing's quite as threatening. The sounds and smells make you feel much closer to the outdoors. And God, the money everywhere. It's obvious there's more than enough to go around. You must have thought about writing movies, right?

Wish you could see me in my tiny two-piece. Better yet, wish you could see me without it. Can't wait to be with you again—even if it means coming back there to the slush and slime. Gotta go.

xxxxxxxxxxxxxxxxxxxxxxxxx + x,
(1 for every hour of the day + 1 for anywhere you want)
Andee

P.S. The tennis pro says I'm pretty good. But then again, he couldn't seem to keep his eye on the ball. Think you could? (That's what they all say . . .) Just watch out, I'm ready for you, playwright.

Tuesday, January 31

Mr. David Raskov
DR Productions
Producers 11, Suite 6B
The Burbank Studios
Burbank, CA 91505

Dear David:

As per our conversation yesterday, here is a brief synopsis of the Richard Case novel in progress. I think it may be the story we're looking for. Keep in mind that I know only the bare bones of the plot at this point and I have not told Case I am doing this. I have reason to believe he wouldn't mind, though, and I think you'll agree it's more than enough for submission. Working title: *My Wife's Affair*.

The setting is the PRESENT. Any major metropolitan area in America. TED and DIANE are a bright young couple, mid-thirties, good-looking. Life has been good to them and they have much of what they set out to capture when they met and married just out of college. But as our story begins they have been prone to bouts of depression and fighting that neither can explain. DIANE thinks it's because they turned their backs on the ideals they once held dear. TED thinks her refusal to "grow up" and let go of those ideals is more to the point.

We see them have an enormous fight one night amid the splendor of their clean designer furnishings and TED walks out of the house and spends the night in a motel. When he calls DIANE at her office in the morning and the fight resumes over the telephone, he decides to take a

72

room of his own in town. Hard as it may be to believe, he is happier with nothing but a bare room in the city than he was in his house full of possessions in the suburbs.

We see both him and DIANE adjusting to being without each other. Some of the new freedoms are liberating; some are confining. Each goes out with other people, with mixed results, some of them comic and some serious. In spite of these affairs—and maybe in Ted's case, because of them—we see them inch toward wanting to see each other again. Finally TED calls DIANE and asks her for a "date." She likes the sound of the idea and agrees to it.

They meet for dinner in town and talk as though they are new to one another. Each expresses likes and dislikes, sometimes to the surprise of the other. By being with new people, they have both remembered how to speak up as though the other person needs to get to know them. They clearly enjoy this time with each other, but at the end of the evening they kiss and go their separate ways. Perhaps hearing these new things about one another is a bit frightening, even intimidating. But it also renews something that has been missing between them: a sense of challenge.

Thus begins their new courtship. Each enjoys this new ritual of dating and romance, and soon it grows into a relationship each is having fun with again. They meet in funny little restaurants and bars. They go to midnight showings of movies. They send each other gifts and write love letters as though they were kids. Then they take a room in a hotel one night and sleep with each other again. The adventure is enticing and the strange place heightens the experience. They find themselves doing this again and again. And sometimes in places where they might be caught in the act. Both find the experiences exhilarating. Man and wife are having an affair—only it is with each other.

And through the affair we see them learn to appreciate each other again. They share secrets that have been locked in forever. They express desires long abandoned as hopeless. They sometimes fight but with a new openness that allows each to make demands that don't threaten the other selfishly. They even write each other letters, something they haven't done in years. A new enthusiasm is born in their lives and it shows in all areas, including work.

Finally TED feels the time has come to proclaim their new existence to the world. He asks DIANE to marry him again—even though they are still man and wife. She agrees and we leave them at their second wedding, reborn, reestablished, and again in love.

I see this as a film with crossover potential between young and old, the primary market being the *Big Chill* audience. It is a romance with comic overtones and, of course, offers two great parts to actors in the salable age groups.

I do foresee some problems with making the sale, as it *is* a character story, but it will be a published novel, and the writer's first book, which he adapted himself, is in production on the lot right now. Even so, we might want to go in with actors or a director committed ahead of the deal.

I think this has great potential, David. The story has enormous appeal to yours truly—an occurrence that, as you know, can be called uncommon, at best. Let me know if you want to proceed and then I'll think about how to approach the author.

Best,
Lynn

THE BEVERLY HILLS HOTEL

Wednesday, February 1

Mr. J. J. Towne
c/o Futterman
183 Central Park West
New York, NY 10023

Dear JJ,

Well, it's finally Wednesday, which means we leave for home. I have so many feelings, it would be unfair to even call them mixed. So let me try to confess.

I hope you won't mind, but I took the car this morning and drove by your house. Something inside just told me to do it, and I'm both glad and sorry I did. It isn't that I was disappointed or anything like that. In fact, it was just the opposite. It's such a sweet place, JJ. The sun was shining and the whole canyon seemed like a little world of its own. Birds were singing, it smelled like pine, and I could hear water flowing, though I don't know from where. And your little yard with the white stones leading up to the door looked like an invitation to peace.

I sat in front for the longest time just looking. You know, I've never lived in a house, JJ. When I was growing up in Boston I used to dream of what it would be like. Not even anything special. Just a place where nobody was on the other side of the walls and your door opened to the outside. And sitting there looking at your place— well, it just seemed like a dream that I knew the person who lived there, that I had kissed him and held him in my arms.

But then another car drove up and a guy got out. I guess it was a messenger because he had a big script envelope and a signature book. He rang the bell and the door opened. And even though I had no intention of having anything like this happen, I saw your wife and Rudi, JJ. And then I got really sad. She looks so pretty and smart. She has the most beautiful blond hair and even the messenger gave her a second look as he walked back to his car. And Rudi is everything you say. Her little freckle face and the big white feather tail that didn't stop wagging for a second. They both looked like . . . I don't know, a family. I know you've been honest with me and all, but seeing them in the flesh was so . . . unexpected. Serves me right, I guess, but I just wasn't ready for it. You've got a whole life here and even though you told me about it, I guess it kind of shocked me to see it was for real.

I didn't stay long after that. I turned on the radio and headed back to the hotel. And you know what? I understood for the first time what LA people say about driving time being their therapy. I went from being almost shaky to feeling a new resolve just in the couple of miles back down out of the canyon. We do have lives, JJ, and it isn't going to be easy to leave them behind, but I know I still want to. And I believe the things you told me. In fact, I believe them even more. If you're willing to leave what you have here, then you must be serious, you must really want me. I hope so. As I got down to Sunset, "Every Breath You Take" was playing on the radio and I found myself crying that I meant the words as bad as Sting's voice was screaming them. I want to have you like that, JJ, so that every sound you make, every breath you take, is for me.

We leave in a couple of hours for the airport. I'm sitting on a little bench by the tennis court here at the hotel and I'm scared. Facing Matt is going to be different now. Things seem more real. But I'm going to do it, JJ. For you. And for myself. Because sitting there outside your house like that, even though it hurt, I think I caught a glimpse for the first time of what life could actually be like. And I want to live that way, JJ. I'm hungry for it. And for you.

By the time you read this, I'll be back in your arms.

Love,
Andee

Thursday, February 2

Mr. Richard Case
27 Saltair Road
Malibu, CA 90233

Dear Deek,

Thanks for the letter. Glad you feel so involved in the whole affair. I guess I've always sort of suspected that some of what you say is true—especially the stuff about our friendship—but it's nice to hear it described that way. Anybody ever tell you that you have a way with words?

Andee's been out of town since I last wrote you. She mentioned a daydream about California to Stanese and he ran right out and bought tickets. The guy's too much. So our fantasy of some afternoons together was in the toilet. But she should be back soon. Maybe even today. We'll see what the trip did for her.

I know what it did for me. I've been working like a madman, all juiced, but in my spare time I think I've also relived my entire romantic life since my first day of consciousness. Some sort of taking stock is definitely going on. It's as though my brain is trying to place all sexual encounters on some sort of continuum so I can understand where Andee fits in.

And you want to know something funny? The more I think about it, the more I realize it's one long history of triangles. I've been lying awake nights reaching back into memory to be sure and, try as I may to find otherwise, that's what it seems to add up to.

As near as I can tell, it started on the South Side of Chicago when I was around four years old. (Yes, four . . .)

I used to play doctor up in my bedroom with Linda Becker, my next-door neighbor, and then run over to another block where I'd listen to records with Mary Little, the daughter of one of my father's friends. At that age, being on the next block was, I suppose, the equivalent of being in another city now. Until we all went to school the following year, neither of them knew the other existed.

Then in grammar school I can remember having an enemy every year when I would take some friend's girlfriend away from him. The third side of the triangle was then the injured party, but he was there nevertheless. Later in adolescence, I found myself unbelievably moved over the film of *Doctor Zhivago*, with the good doctor trundling back and forth across the tundra for love of both Geraldine Chaplin and Julie Christie, who was for me the archangel of beauty with her blond hair, rimmed blue eyes, and pouting lips. I immediately recreated this triangle of pain with two girls, one of whom went to my high school, Niles West, while the other (with rimmed blue eyes) went cross town to Niles East. I remember an ugly scene outside a pizza place named Gulliver's when the whole thing came crashing down around me.

I think this continued all the way through college, too, although a turning point appeared when a guy's girlfriend came on to me very heavily and I rejected her because I didn't want to lose his friendship. But it was shortly after that that I met Lynn. And I took her away from a friend who wanted her but encouraged me because she was tempting him to leave the girl *he* planned to marry. And funny enough, the night I remember as a turning point in our relationship, where it went from acquaintance to something more intimate, was when I slipped a note in her pocket with a bunch of triangles on it that turned into two overlapping circles.

I guess the rest is history, or at least what I'm attempting to define as a history. Lynn and I were married two years when we met you at the Drama School and as you well know, neither marriage nor the ivy halls of Yale seemed up to breaking my fascination with the eternal isosceles.

So what do you make of all this, Deek? Am I sick or do I, as you suggest, just act out the baser impulses that we all seem to share? Is it some infantile repetition of a trapping situation designed for me to get caught or is it just that I get bored and find intrigue rejuvenating? Maybe I've got some guilty secret that I long to be punished for. Or maybe I just enjoy a guilty pleasure every now and then. Or maybe I'm just in love with falling in love.

Help me, Doc. If I'm a character in this novel you're writing, you ought to be able to say what makes me tick. (Dare I ask what the book is about at this point?)

Your friend and fictional inspiration,
JJ Towne

P.S. Sorry to hear what they're doing to your movie. Just take the money and run, Deek. Write your new book.

The play, to answer your question, is coming along very well. I think a good triangle acts as a pyramid and attracts energy from the heavens. Hey, maybe that's all there is to it. . .

THE ADVICE OF THE MIRROR

I've begun masturbating again. Which is funny to me. In a nice way. I used to do it all the time as a girl. I considered it almost holy, an act of faith. I would lie in bed at night and pray for Him, ache to meet Him, almost scream at the very thought that He was somewhere on the face of the earth and I didn't know who or where He was. And then my hand would slide inside my pajamas, like God's touch in the dark, to bridge the silent distance between His existence and mine, and as I rose nearer to orgasm I would fantasize that somewhere He was doing the same thing in this moment and even though we had not yet faced each other we were sharing this sensation, sharing our blind desire for each other, coming together in the huge black void of the night.

And then I finally met Him. JJ was him—there was no doubt about it. He even confirmed that I was correct in my girlhood fantasy, that he was with me in those nights of longing, that he used to fuck his pillow and sheets with an identically desperate desire to know me. His brother once told me that JJ in fact used to speak my very thoughts as they were falling asleep on many a night in the room of their childhood—that it was driving him crazy that I was out there and he didn't know who I was yet.

And so, when I met him, I stopped. I was actually embarrassed at the time because masturbation had suddenly become *the* topic of conversation on everyone's lips. It seemed you couldn't pick up a book or magazine or turn on the television or radio without hearing this or that doctor or this or that writer or this or that feminist extolling the virtues of caressing the clit. Self-indulgence was set forth not as sin but as therapy. Mirrors were even prescribed, for observation of the act, as if such an inner pleasure could be reflected in a piece of glass. I rejected this entire notion, considered it almost blasphemy and certainly an insult to the purity of my desire. And I didn't lay a finger on myself for years. JJ was all I needed. He was all I had ever asked for. His touch gave me the chills. I once came the instant one of his fingers slid between my legs. Surely this was not just physical sensation. It was an answered prayer.

But then last weekend out at the beach, Deek asked me to do something with him. We had already eaten dinner and fucked and eaten a late night lover's snack of oatmeal cookies and milk. And he took me by the hand and led me back into his bedroom where he revived a fire we had built hours earlier to make the room as heated as we were. And he sat me down naked on a pillow in front of the fire. And he sat himself naked on an identical pillow facing me. And he asked me to masturbate with him. And to see if we could come at the same time. Without so much as touching one another. Except with our eyes. No speaking even. Just our eyes.

And I did this. For the first time in my life with a man. And it was one of the most intense sexual experiences I have ever had. For a while I felt we were actually levitating above the fire. We had done no drugs. This was no 60's love encounter. It was two human beings sharing perhaps the most private act they could allow another to witness. And sharing it freely. And with conviction. I remember thinking at one point while I was staring into his eyes, really staring, that this was not even sex, that it was telepathic communication, like the silent screams of longing I used to send out into the night as a girl in search of JJ. In fact, it was somehow as though JJ was there too.

I am not in love with Deek. I was not in love with

82

him that night. But he does have an extraordinary quality of understanding about him. You sense you can trust him immediately. And that there need be no secrets. He is so in control that you sense he has even created the time that encloses you in such a moment with him. Or that he is creating you in the moment. And oddly enough, you don't mind. You even welcome this control, as though it is a relief from the burden of living.

But as I said, as we faced each other, at one point, I felt that JJ was there. I don't know who he occurred to first—Deek or me—but he materialized in our stares and jumped back and forth like an electric arc and I think for a time it was he who caressed both of us. And the danger of this idea overlapped with the danger of our real fears and, as I now remember it, the fire briefly dimmed. But then Deek willed JJ away, perhaps as easily as he willed him into existence, and our eyes were once again fixed on each other. And we leaned closer and wanted to but did not touch. And hands were everywhere. And mouths opened. And the fire reared up. And backs arched. Legs tensed. Lungs filled. And we came. Both of us. Together.

And then the lock of our gaze melted. And we were suddenly upon each other. And I can't remember ever feeling that human flesh burned so hot. Our stomachs were glued together by our heat and we held each other for the longest time without making a sound. Our breathing was all there was to human existence. And then Deek whispered something in my ear to break the silence.

"I saw your soul," he said.

Then we slept. Like gods who had watched the results of their whim come to physical life on an earth below them. Without regret. And when I awoke in the morning we were still stuck in our embrace, our bodies clinging together like two inspired ideas, each enamored of the other.

I smiled. And Deek smiled. Even Rudi smiled. Then I

was back in my car, and back here at home. Where I have repeated my experience many times this week. In my mind. And body. And I feel I have finally taken the advice of the mirror. Only my mirror was and is (for now) Deek. I, too, saw my soul. When I looked. When he did. And I didn't mind what I saw.

DOWN BY THE RIVER

Thursday, February 2

Mr. J. J. Towne
c/o Futterman
183 Central Park West
New York, NY 10023

JJ—

I'm back. Have to see you. Dot's place, tomorrow, 1:15?
Bring your toothbrush.

Love you,
Andee

Thursday, February 2

Maggie Steinfeld
170 Thompson Street, #3
New York, NY 10012

Dear Maggie,

I couldn't leave things like that and since I'm not used to people hanging up telephones on me, I thought I'd just drop you a note.

First off, let's get something straight. I don't enjoy fucking up people's lives. Or their schedules for even one afternoon. I apologize about tomorrow. I wouldn't have canceled on you unless it was absolutely necessary. I know I probably sounded a little vague, but I assure you something important has come up and there's just no way I can get around it. If I knew how long it was going to take, I would gladly meet you afterward, but the fact is I don't. You'll just have to trust me.

Look, things have been great between us. I've appreciated every ounce of support you've sent my way. The play's coming fabulously. We're going to have our new draft soon. As well as our shot at everything we're both looking for. A major production. Broadway. So let's not blow this all out of proportion. It's one lunch. I promise you, I'll make it up to you. Let's say we've had our first fight and leave it at that. Deal?

Call me. Write me. Whatever you prefer. I learned a long time ago to use pencil on my calendar when it comes to the theater. I'll be here.

JJ

Friday night, late, February 3

Miss Andee O'Neill
c/o "Down by the River"
Warwick Studios
5460 Seventh Ave.
New York, NY 10020

Dear Andee,

After an experience like that, words seem ridiculous. And yet words are all I have for company tonight. I want you here with me, right now, and I try in vain to recreate you, to make you materialize, with words. And I am struck by the futility of the task. This should be the moment when a writer is most grateful for his skills, for all the years put in, for all the practice at bringing places, people, moments of time, alive. And yet it is just the opposite. A true longing for the reality of a human being, wanting them by your side, now, exposes the craft of writing for what it is—a sham, a trick, a hopeless arranging and rearranging of memories in a vain attempt at bringing thoughts, emotions, people, to life.

I can remember a kiss and place it on a character's lips. And then I can locate that character in a setting which lends validity to the telling of the kiss. And I can even make my reader breathe as I did when I tasted the kiss. But do I have the kiss? No. If I have been clever in my description, I have something that suggests the life of the kiss. But it is not real life or the real kiss. It is, if I am any good, a heartfelt regret for the passing of the time of the kiss, which then recreates my regret in the heart of my reader, who tonight, sadly, is only me.

87

Your touch is still all over me. So is your scent. And (forgive my smile) it feels like my first time. . . . And I keep flashing on that too.

It was the summer between my junior and senior years in high school and Mick Jagger was singing "Time Is on My Side" on the radio and I was with my best friend's girl on a steamy Chicago night when her parents were out of town. I didn't understand it at the time and, to be honest, I'm not sure I do now, but I think she and my friend had reached the point in their relationship when it was time to sleep together and yet they hadn't, and the pressure was so overwhelming that she needed to some-how release it. And yet she didn't want to sleep with my friend because of the way that would advance the state of things between them (i.e., she would have to keep sleep-ing with him). But she also couldn't stand the pressure of her virginity. And then along came me. I was attracted to her, no doubt about that. If it wasn't my best friend who she was involved with, I'd have made a move on her much sooner. But it was. And I felt awful about it. But not awful enough to say no.

It was her idea. As we were all going home from the Dairy Queen in Lincolnwood (our local hang), she whis-pered to me that I should come over after I dropped everyone off. I smiled and asked why and she put a hand on my thigh and the adrenaline started pumping. I thought twice about it but my adolescent hormones got the better of me, and before I knew it I was dropping off my friend and then driving back to her house, climbing her steps, and knocking on her door. No more than ten minutes later we were flat on her couch out in this dark converted den off her living room with bamboo roll blinds and she was french-kissing me and tugging at a stubborn zipper on my jeans. It came loose with a jerk, as did I, and after some more wrestling with clothes we were fumbling with the ultimate threshold in a young life, both of us terrified and amazed that we were actually going to pass through it. I remember the softness and the wetness and how dark it was and how hot her tongue felt in my mouth and how her nipples pushed into the palms of my hands with surprising hardness and how even after it was all over I could feel every sensation again and again as we lay there breathing into each other's ears.

And then when I stumbled into my clothes and my car after saying my clumsy not understanding good-byes and found my way back to my house and my own bed in a darkness that seemed more alive than I had ever known darkness could be, I finally allowed myself the private smile that every young boy knows, and I remember just lying there in the night smelling the sex on my body, feeling its touch on my skin, and thinking I was part of the world and alive.

Which is how I feel tonight. And Mick Jagger is still on the radio, only now he's singing "Memory Motel," and I'm sitting here at this moment a registered guest in that abode, and I'm a tape recorder searching for the sounds of human heartbeats and I've found one. Or two. I listened to them today when I laid my head across your breast. And I'm listening to them tonight here at my desk. And I'm happy again. And sexed again. And alive again.

And I think I'll stop with the futility of words again. And just get into bed and savor your smell. And your feel. Like that young boy in his teenage night. And like him, I'll resolve never to take a shower again, so as not to wash this dream of your love away. That boy betrayed no one that hot summer night. He only opened himself to his own desire. And in doing so, learned one of life's lessons— that such desires, if we act on them, will almost always bring us into conflict with the world. I'm open tonight, Andee. To the same desire. And the same conflict. We're

89

partners in love. And in crime. Which makes it just like the first time. Which suits me just fine.

Good night.
JJ

Saturday, February 4

Mr. J. J. Towne
c/o Futterman
183 Central Park West
New York, NY 10023

JJ—

Be careful. I think Matt knows something. I'm afraid.

Andee

Saturday, February 4

What was that about? JJ calls for the first time in a week or more and sounds like a soldier going to meet his death. If anything happens to me, he says, you'll remember the way I loved you, right? Right, I say. But what am I saying? And why? It can't be the play. He says he's into the second act and it couldn't be going better. It must be what I already know, that he is not coming back. It probably gave him a brief moment of panic, his haunting fear of height. He probably looked out his own window, saw himself splattered on the sidewalk below, and picked up the phone as if to apologize for climbing out onto the ledge he has decided to call home. And I am kind to him. Supportive. I talk him back inside. Being careful not to press. God forbid I should demand an explanation. Or even ask for one politely. It is a line I am not allowed to cross. And dutifully, I do not.

And I think how different it is with Deek. I can say anything. The more probing my questions, the more he seems to appreciate my mind. And then he reciprocates. And the thrusts end up feeling like sex instead of weapons.

My God . . . Deek. . . . Maybe JJ knows. . . . It never occurred to me.

92

Saturday, February 4

Mr. J. J. Towne
c/o Futterman
183 Central Park West
New York, NY 10023

Hey, buddy—

Just got a strange call from Lynn, who apparently got a strange call from you. . . . Is everything all right? I tried you all morning but nobody seems to be picking up the phone there. This should reach you tomorrow, if overnight really means overnight as those puddyfaces on the tube claim.

Give me a buzz, huh? Maybe you need to talk? I'm here.

Deek

DOT PENNER

Mr. J. J. Towne
c/o Futterman
183 Central Park West
New York, NY 10023

JJ—

If you're not busy tomorrow night, the Rabbit and I would like to have you over to our place for one of his blue-ribbon pasta dinners. He also says he wants to talk to you, and though he won't tell me what about, I get the feeling it's Andee. (I haven't said anything but it probably wasn't real smart of her to pick up the phone when you guys were here yesterday. . . .)
    Anyway, around 7:30, okay?

Love,
Dot

P.S. Don't worry, I'll protect you.

DOT PENNER

Maggie Steinfeld
170 Thompson Street, #3
New York, NY 10012

Dear Mag,

Your service says you're away for the weekend. Give me a call when you get back, huh?

I think our boy may have worked himself into a corner that is going to make it difficult for him to stick around town in the near future. Naturally I'm concerned, and I think it might not be a bad idea for you to subtly ask to see some pages at this point (i.e., before we extend our investment in either time and/or bucks).

The Rabbit and I are having him over for dinner tomorrow night, so I'll talk to you after that.

Hope your being away means good news from New Haven.

Best,
Dot

Sunday, February 5

Mr. Richard Case
27 Saltair Road
Malibu, CA 90233

Dear Deek,

Got your note and just tried to call you. Naturally your
machine was beneficiary to my ramblings. I love this—it's
starting to feel like an Ibsen play where notes and messages delivered to drawing rooms signal major events
swirling just offstage in matters of the heart. Maybe the
telephone answering machine's indirect gift to the modern
world will be a return of the delicate tension of waiting for
the next word. Anyway, please forgive the disoriented
quality of my message. It's been one of those weeks . . .

Stanese is on to me and Andee. She says he didn't
pick up on anything while they were in California, but she
wrote me letters every day and even took their car for a
spin by my place while he was supposedly holed up in
the Polo Lounge cracking his knuckles over West Coast
"business." And you have to believe that a guy with his
penchant for claiming ownership of his little lady doesn't
miss too many tricks. I know he saw her writing the
letters. I only hope he didn't read them. (She likes to talk
about what her tongue is going to do to me when I next
come in contact with it. . . .)

Naturally we figured out a way to get together when
she got back. Dot Penner loaned us her place for the
afternoon on Friday and suffice it to say we were happy to
see each other and we expressed our happiness physi-
cally. But while we're there the phone rings and Andee

96

picks it up thinking it might be Dot calling from the show. Someone is breathing on the other end but isn't saying anything, so she hangs up. We get appropriately nervous but after about eight seconds we fall back into never-never land.

Of course Friday night is a drag. I'm sitting alone in Futterman's palace smelling two and a half hours of ecstasy all over my body and she's down in SoHo frying up the Ragu. Then Saturday morning I go out for some eggs at one of the eighteen Greek diners within my morning tolerance for walking and while I'm sitting there with *The Times*, this guy in a smooth charcoal suit wanders over and gives me a big pat on the back.

"How you doing, JJ Towne?" he says with this shit-eating grin on his pretty-boy face.

And I say fine, but then admit that I don't remember where we've made our acquaintance.

"Really?" Pretty Boy asks in amazement. "I'm a good friend of Matt Stanese's."

"Yeah?" I ask, half ready to be belligerent and half terrified that his free hand is going to disappear beneath his coat and come out with a pair of cement shoes in my size, or a one-way ticket home, or worse.

But Pretty Boy just stands there smiling and says only, "Amazing how small a world New York can be, isn't it?"

"Yeah." I smile back, now afraid that the yellow of my egg which has turned to crust on my tongue is going to fall out of my mouth like a tombstone. I can see the headline in the *Post*: L.A. PLAYWRIGHT CHOKES ON HIS OWN WORDS.

But Pretty Boy is doing the talking and I deign to listen. "Yeah, I might just be out for a stroll on Central Park West," he intones like he's remembering streets from his youth with fondness, "or maybe I'm over at the fruit stand at Columbus and 73rd buying apples, Granny Smiths, or the Häagen-Dazs up at 75th picking up some mocha almond fudge to take home with me, or even down the avenue at this Japanese place, Lenge, dropping yellowtail down my throat, no mustard in my soy sauce, when sure enough I can run into the person I'd least expect to see in the entire city. It's just amazing. . . ."

My knees are now knocking under the table. Pretty Boy, who looks like he could offer up the Lord's Prayer and/or a switchblade on his next breath, has just recited in exquisite detail the basic stops on my upper west side afternoon itinerary for the past month. Christ, he's even been close enough to see that I don't put the green mustard in my soy sauce at Lenge. Obviously he's seen what else has gone into my mouth in this lovely little Japanese hang (i.e., Andee O'Neill's tongue).

Not knowing what to utter as last words, I shrug and say, "Yeah, it's quite a city. Nothing like it on the coast." And at this, he and I know I am scared shitless. No one from LA refers to home as "the coast." It would be like a native San Franciscan saying "Frisco." Or somebody from NaHaven actually saying "New" and "Haven" as though they were two words.

So Pretty Boy pats me on the back again. And smiles again. This time looking through my eyes like an X-ray probe checking out the inner surface of my skull. Message delivered. Message received. Incredible how unnecessary words are after the proper words have been spoken. The playwright in me made a note of this even as my teeth began to chatter, for as I saw his charcoal suit disappear among the preppie cardigans, Timberlands, and baby carriages outside the diner, I knew I would live to tell the tale.

I was afraid to go back to Futterman's for the rest of the day, but I'm here now, twelve hours of night have come and gone, and as far as I can tell, my existence was verified at breakfast when Futterman asked me how the work was coming. I'm not sure he appreciated my laugh, but I know you will once you've received this. Just promise me, Deek, that if I disappear, or they find me floating facedown in the East River, that you'll exact revenge, that you'll spirit Miss O'Neill into the night and marry her happily ever after in Malibu, where you'll both pray for my eternal salvation before you fuck your brains out every night.

I've been invited to Dot Penner's for dinner tonight. Supposedly the Rabbit wants to offer me a home-cooked meal, but it feels more like when the Rosato brothers offer Frankie Five Angels the C-note before they try to strangle him in *The Godfather*. So I'll drop this in the mail to you now, Deek, in case it's the last anyone ever hears of me. Save it as evidence. And remember, you have been charged with a holy mission—my revenge and sexual salvation.

Your brother in blood,
JJ Towne

So much for my imagination . . . I race over to Deek's wearing the blinders of a lover's fear, thinking we have been discovered, and after Deek has reassured me that there is no basis at all for such an assumption (the reassurance coming in the form of his tongue and my removed pair of 501's lying in a heap at the end of his bed), the telephone rings and via the wonderful modern convenience of the answering machine, JJ's voice materializes in the room. Understand, I am lying in a bed by the sea with a man who has just performed cunnilingus on me and we are drifting in and out of consciousness with the sound of each wave outside the window, when an electronically amplified voice begins to speak and it is the voice of my husband. Afterward Deek said one couldn't write such a scene into even a sentimental movie—it would not be believed.

But a scene it was. And I think that in the middle of it Deek was tempted to get up and switch off the volume as though it *were* part of a bad movie. Certainly afterward we both wished the machine had been set that way, or not set at all, but once it started, once JJ began talking to us as though an invisible presence in the room, we both froze, like still-lifes caught in the malicious flash of a spying camera.

But Deek found a way to break the spell. After JJ hung up he said we imagined the whole thing, that we'd allowed our worst paranoid delusions to get the better of us in guilt over our bliss. And to prove it, he stood and rewound the tape. Sure enough, when he played it through a second time it was blank as leader. The nasty hiss of recorded nothingness defied us to say that memory was more accurate than Memorex. It hung there in the air like Deek's smile, and so, of course, I played along. It was far easier than dealing with the reality of JJ's interruption, and I find that when people are naked from the waist down, as I was, reality is often the last thing they want on their minds. Deek had erased the tape like an emperor of old dispatching the bearer of bad tidings to the executioner's chopping block, and for the moment at least we were free of the unfortunate coincidence of JJ's bad timing.

Of course I thought about it later, as I was driving home. These drives are getting to be like reentry trajectories anyway, where I am jolted in stages back to the reality of my earthbound existence, but this one was an exception even as jolts go.

I felt the heat when I turned off the Pacific Coast Highway onto Sunset. But it was not LA heat. It was the heat from within. The adrenaline. The advance warning that arrives in the night like an unwelcome knock on the door and tells you the fun is on its way. That's what you learn to call an anxiety attack—fun—because something that awful must owe its place in the world to *someone's* enjoyment. If not, the devil exists and God is helpless before him.

Following the heat came the chills. And the nausea. The disorientation and pounding of blood in the ears. I pulled over. This was surely death, striking out of the blue. Or out of the ocean, which sat like a picture postcard in the rearview mirror above me. I hadn't had one of these attacks in a long time. I'd told myself I was over them. They've plagued me on and off over the years, mostly in times of stress, but sometimes at equally opposite moments of total peace. I've seen shrinks about them. And behavioral scientists. Even chemists, who have promised it is my blood and not me that is responsible. But when one of these things hits you, it's not responsibility you're interested in. It's breathing. There is no sense to anxiety. Only an eternal struggle to return it to the place from whence it came.

I managed to survive. As always. And I managed to get myself home. Certainly it was JJ's call that prompted my fit. Any amateur psychobabble artist would say so. But somehow I can't convince myself that it's quite that simple. Anxiety isn't understood so quickly. I've been thinking about it all evening, in fact, and here is what I've come up with.

When JJ called on Deek's machine, it would have been bad enough if he had just said that it was him and asked Deek to call back. But he didn't. He talked on, as though he was in a stupor, jumping from thought to thought almost incoherently for well over a minute. I don't know whether something was wrong or whether it was just JJ leaving the kind of strange rambling message he enjoys filling people's answer tapes with, but his voice burned in my ears not only with the disappointment of the moment, but of recent years as well. JJ definitely has a style. He's had it since I first met him. But as time goes by and his hopes and dreams keep sinking in slow motion through the quicksand of the real world, it is beginning to wear thin. His voice on that machine was no longer charming in its disjointedness. It was only disjointed. His attempts at humor were no longer innocent in the way they fell just short of their mark. They were burdened with time's weight and a sense that they would never make their target, never arrive at the laugh. God knows I've believed in him over the years. But whereas someone like Deek makes an inability to fit in into a life that ends up working for him, JJ only continues to make his life into an inability to fit in.

I am attracted to the odd man out. I always have been. But as I grow older I am experiencing the paradox of that attraction—that wanting that man and living with him are two entirely different matters. Spending this time with Deek is, to be sure, bringing the terrain into a sharper focus. It is forcing me to admit that I like the pose of the outsider, not the real thing. The man who knows disgust from having been inside the walls, not the one who has the anger of the beggar turned away at the door.

I've loved JJ. I've loved him well. But though my sympathies are with the down-and-outers on the planet, I guess I never planned on spending my life in their company. It isn't money that I want, but neither is it the netherworld I've been assigned to. I feel I'm being brave to admit it, even if it is a little late and only to myself here in this notebook. Maybe this distance JJ and I have put between us right now is there for a reason then, so that I can see it for what it is—the honest distance between our hopes and our lives. I don't know what it would take to close such a distance either. Maybe if the play actually happens. Or if I come out of this affair with Deek knowing something I do not now foresee. A part of me still wants my marriage to survive. Another part says its day is already well in the past. I embrace all sides of myself here in this house tonight, but I feel like a figure in a jigsaw puzzle who is growing tired of not having all my pieces in place, who knows it's getting harder and harder to wait. I no longer feel I have an infinite amount of patience. Or strength.

What is beyond patience, JJ? What is beyond strength? What I fear most. Fear itself. And its ever-present shadow. Anxiety.

PETER FUTTERMAN

Sun., 2/5

Dear JJ,

As you know, I have to go out to California tomorrow for a few days and since I may not see you when you get back tonight from Dot's, I wanted to just leave you with a few thoughts.

Maggie called me earlier this evening and expressed some concern about when we would be seeing the re-write. I don't know if anything has happened between the two of you, but she sounded as though she was suddenly having some reservations about the project. Apparently Dot Penner shares this concern and presumably she is discussing it with you tonight.

This is news to me, JJ, and frankly I would have preferred to hear it from you. I will give you the benefit of the doubt, though, as judging from the hours I see you put in at that desk and your seeming enthusiasm about the work you're doing, I find it hard to believe that anything could be wrong—at least from your point of view.

I know Maggie somewhat better than you do and it is my experience that she is prone to excessive worrying at times. This comes with the territory of a young director, I find, and though I do not care for manufactured crises (there are enough real ones to deal with in this business), I continue to believe in her for this project. If, however, anything has happened between the two of you, I would appreciate knowing about it. Perhaps this was the reason for your laughter at breakfast yesterday?

As you are aware, JJ, Susie and I have grown quite

fond of having you with us in our home over the past weeks. The more I know of you, the more faith I have in you as a person and as a writer. I think this play has enormous potential. But I must believe that you are being honest with me about your progress. I haven't put the pressure of any deadlines on you—I don't believe that is the way to work in the theater—and as a guest in our apartment you are as easy and delightful as anyone who has ever stayed with us. But I would like your assurance that we are moving forward as anticipated. If Maggie is a problem, then we will need to make alternate plans, though that would be sticky at this stage. I don't know where Dot Penner fits in. Though she claims to want to produce on this project, she hasn't spoken with me.

So please let me know, JJ. Perhaps I have misinterpreted your quietness at times and should have pressed more for progress reports. I will be at the Beverly Hills Hotel through Wednesday night. If we don't talk by phone, let's plan on dinner Thursday when I get back.

Fondly,
Peter

THE WYNDHAM HOTEL
42 West 58th St.
New York, New York 10019

Sunday night, February 5

Lynn Towne
DR Productions
Producers 11, Suite 6B
The Burbank Studios
Burbank, CA 91505

Lynn—

I took the memo on the Case novel, *My Wife's Affair*, with me on the plane, and as I find myself still thinking about it after a cross-country flight, a dinner with Paul Cohn, a truly shallow evening in the theater (Broadway . . .), and a nightcap alone in my room, I thought I'd just jot down a few random notes and pass them along to you.

1) How long a time span are we talking about over the course of the breaking apart of this couple, their various flings with others, their reestablishing contact, their affair with each other, and their second wedding vows?

2) Do we get to know any of the others they have affairs with or is this part just blind sex? (The latter, I hope.)

3) Do we get a sense of this couple's past? If so, how?

4) Would a married couple really be able to fall in love a second time?

106

5) How would the sex be between them when they get back together?

6) How was it before? (i.e., was this part of their problem?)

7) Do you think sex is possible within a marriage?

8) How about without? (Just kidding . . .)

9) Is love something that can start up again after it stops? And does it ever really stop between these two?

10) In a time when marriage is again becoming the socially desirable pursuit, is a movie questioning its values going to disturb people or reassure them?

11) Which would you rather do?

12) Who do you see in these parts?

13) Would kids stay away from this movie? (I hope so.)

14) Would it still make money for Coca-Cola? (i.e., what would be their reason for funding it? i.e., could our couple take the Pepsi challenge in the film and prefer Coke?)

15) Is lust something you can feel for someone after it has disappeared for even a minute in a relationship?

16) Is marriage at all dependent on lust?

17) How about lust on marriage?

18) Would men and women answer this question differently?

19) Does that influence who we select to write the script?

20) Does my track record with marriage mean I should disqualify myself from producing it?

21) How are things between you and JJ?

22) Didn't you say he was here in New York now?

23) Will you marry me if he stays?

24) Would this movie get me back here? (i.e., permanently but with the option to make more movies just a phone call away)

25) If this book isn't even written yet, how do you know so much about it?

26) Will the author be amenable to selling us the rights prior to publication?

27) How about after?

28) Should we wait until the film of his first book comes out before approaching him?

29) Should we just steal his story and make our own movie?

30) Regardless of whose story we use, will there be any food fights in the film?

A posthaste reply to any or all of the above will be greatly appreciated. I need something to read on the plane home, you know.

I'm drunk.

Good night.

David

DOWN BY THE RIVER

Monday, February 6, 8 AM

Mr. J. J. Towne
c/o Futterman
183 Central Park West
New York, NY 10023

JJ—

I heard about your dinner last night. Matt got two phone
calls around 11:00. I know one was from Rabbit. I'm not
sure about the other. Matt's giving me the silent treat-
ment, which usually means he's thinking about doing
something stupid. I'm scared. I wish I could see you, but I
can't think how. I have the letter that you wrote me Friday
night right here in my hand and I keep reading it over and
over again. And it affects me the same way as the one you
wrote me while I was in California—every time I read it I
get hotter and weaker. Except you're not here to watch,
like you were on Friday. You're not here to grab and hold
and make the love of my life to. Oh, JJ, *you're* my first
time. I've never felt anything like this. Tell me what to do
and I'll do it.

Love,
Andee

Monday, February 6, 10 AM

Miss Andee O'Neill
c/o "Down by the River"
Warwick Studios
5460 Seventh Ave.
New York, NY 10020

Dear Andee,

I just got your note but unfortunately I don't know what to tell you. Not only did the Rabbit deliver me a sermon last night, but one of your boyfriend's smoothies sat down with me for a little breakfast confession Saturday morning in the diner across from The Dakota where I usually have my hangover eggs. He's been watching us, Andee. He saw us at Lenge and I don't know where else.

I have your letters here in front of me and they make me want you all the more too. But we know what we're up against now. Listening to Pretty Boy over in the diner was a very sobering experience. Probably similar to what you went through outside my house when you found yourself looking at Lynn. And last night at Dot's, with Rabbit squeezing me—it didn't scare me but it did make me think about just how much we would have to go through to make this thing real.

So I don't really know. I was up most of last night but I can't figure it. Maybe we should run away. On the other hand, maybe we should back off for now. At least as a disguise tactic. I'm not looking to get my face bloodied, which seems to be the message I'm receiving here. And I certainly don't want anything to happen to you. Also, Futterman's out of town for a few days and I've decided I

110

have to finish the play by the time he gets back. So how about if we just lay low and see if some time will help us? Then if I'm on Broadway and you're ready for films, who's going to stop us from making our move?

Maybe our time is yet to come, that's all. If so, I'll be ready. Whenever. There's no forgetting you, Andee.

I love you.

JJ

Mr. Peter Futterman
c/o The Beverly Hills Hotel
9641 West Sunset Blvd.
Beverly Hills, CA 90210

Dear Peter,

I was quite upset to get your note last night and I'm sorry you were asleep when I got back to the apartment. I would have preferred to speak with you before you left, but I'll send this out express mail and hopefully it will hold us both over until our dinner on Thursday.

First of all, I'm very surprised that Maggie would make such a phone call to you. Something did happen, but it was this: I canceled lunch with her on Friday. It had nothing whatsoever to do with the play or anything that has passed between us regarding the play. I just couldn't do the lunch, and I told her so, on Thursday night.

Well, she went crazy, Peter. She started talking about people who don't keep their word, and how much time and energy she has given this project already, and how she likes to keep to a schedule and it's driving her nuts that we're not really on one yet, and when is the script going to be ready, etc., etc., etc. Maybe this is "the excessive worrying" you describe in your note; to me it is one of the "manufactured crises." I don't honestly know where it came from either. We've been talking practically every day and we've changed plans before. But suddenly missing one lunch means to her that we're going to miss on everything here.

Dot Penner did have a few words to say to me about it, but it was something else altogether. She hears Maggie is being offered another show and she may want out of ours. So perhaps a little "crisis" would be a convenient modus operandi for desertion. I don't know if this is true. I do know that Dot is concerned about it and that she very much thinks of herself as involved in this project. She hasn't spoken with you for the same reason you mention with regard to me—she doesn't want you to feel pressured into having her along; she wants to be welcomed when the time is right.

So, Peter, I don't know what more to say. You're correct in gauging my attitude as an enthusiastic one. I'm very excited about the writing I've been doing and I'm very nearly finished. I've been thriving here in your home and I think being in New York during this phase of the writing is only helping the play. I feel very close to you, and Susie too. It hasn't been often in my life (or my career) that I've felt such a kinship with another couple. Or the comfort that comes of knowing one is so thoroughly believed in. Your accepting my quietness about what I am doing has been, to me, the ultimate gesture of your confidence in me. I promise you, I will not let you down.

As for Maggie, I'm just not sure. I wrote a note to apologize about the canceled lunch right after I spoke with her last Thursday. Apparently neither my call nor the letter did much good. I, too, continue to think she is right for this play in some ways. But not if it means this kind of erupting behind people's backs. I don't function well in that kind of situation, Peter. I think we could all do without it.

But let's wait until you get back to deal with that. By then the whole thing may have blown over. In the meantime, enjoy yourself in our hotel out there. You have the

113

number if you feel like calling Lynn. I know she'd be thrilled to meet you.

Look forward to seeing you Thursday.

Sincerely,
JJ

Monday night, February 6, 3 AM

Mr. Richard Case
27 Saltair Road
Malibu, CA 90233

Dear Deek,

When last I wrote, I remember I thought I might be writing my last. I was on my way to Dot Penner's for dinner, unsure if I would ever return. Let me pick it up right there.

It was freezing as I came out of the building onto Central Park West. Even to a Chicago boy, it was cold. Futterman's doorman (who, after a month of showing him my key, is finally willing to concede that I am living here) seemed to smile as he opened the door for me, so I should have guessed. But I didn't, and the wind sucker-punched me before I even had the zipper on my jacket up. Frostbite of the chest. Gives you a cold heart, my friend. But I had your letter in my breast pocket and I planned to drop it in the box at the corner before I hid my face behind the obligatory woolen scarf.

Once I made the deposit (the mailbox was so frozen that the swinging door didn't even try to take a bite out of my hand) I headed over toward Columbus Avenue on 75th. The ground was caked with snow, making everything quiet as only snow can in this city, and as I walked the short block I thought to myself that I could live on this street, that it was like a New York street seen only in the romantic black and white movies that I used to watch on television as a kid. Snow fell lightly and sparkled in halos

115

around wrought iron streetlamps. A woman walked a dog with a red plaid coat on its back and actually acknowledged me as I passed. Cars sat silent, snow piling up like cake frosting on their windshields. And couples read books by fireplaces behind the Levolorred windows of beautifully renovated brownstones. I looked inside as many windows as I could, amazed to see things like computers, color TVs, halogen lamps, books, and oil paintings.

At Columbus, couples were making their way in and out of the cafés. A girl inside Ruelles smiled at me through the window. People tried to jump the puddles of slush when the lights changed at the crosswalks. And I watched my feet squish through the snow as I headed for the Seventh Avenue subway down at 72nd Street.

I like riding the subway in the winter, especially on a night like this when everyone seems almost grateful for the warmth in the crowding. Up at 96th, where I got off to head over to Dot's town house on West End, it felt even colder out, so I was glad to carry the station's smells, even the foul ones, in my lungs as I leaned into the wind.

When I rang the bell, I knew what kind of night I was in for when Dot opened the door and rolled her eyes to the ceiling before she even said hello. The Rabbit was behind her in the kitchen, pressing garlic near a saucepan. I kicked the snow off my boots, rubbed my nose warm, and walked inside. It smelled fantastic and I thought to myself, at least I'll enjoy my last meal. And then the Rabbit hopped over to me.

"JJ, come in," he said, beaming, "I've got something special for you."

"So soon?" I cracked. "You could at least let me sample the pesto."

"Such a sense of smell," the Rabbit joked. "Where did you get it?"

"We know our food in California," I answered. "That and our natural disasters."

116

The Rabbit seemed to like that. He grinned slyly and said, "A wonderful combination."

I stripped off my coat. And my boots. And my sweater. I think I have more trouble with the heat indoors here than the cold on the streets. But the Rabbit was presenting me with his specialty which, much to my relief, was a platter of mushrooms stuffed with veal, bread crumbs, scallions, and mozzarella. I took a deep breath, popped one in my mouth, and smiled as it went down. If this was death, then I was ready to accept it.

It turned out to be only an appetizer, of course. The prelude to a meal that, I have to admit, was one of the finest I've had since I've been here (were it not for the conversation that accompanied it). Naturally the Rabbit dusted off some of his choice Peruvian flake for the occasion too. So by the time we were winding pasta around our forks, we were as numb-nosed as downhill skiers and probably as hyped.

Two or three hearty mouthfuls later, as I swigged some white Bordeaux and smiled at Dot across the table from me, the Rabbit came right to the point.

"So you've been fucking Baby Andee," he sneered as he wiped dripping pesto from his upper lip. "In spite of what I told you. And right here in my bed."

Dot's smile drained from her face and I thought it was going to be close to see which one of us choked to death first.

"Honey," she managed to cough out at the Rabbit in her best southern, straight from *Down by the River*, exclamatory voice.

"What?" he shot back. "Certainly JJ knows why he is here."

"He's here for a meal," Dot insisted, anger now adding a special hue to the choking red in her cheeks.

"Of course he is," the Rabbit went on, "but since

117

he's already intimate with the surroundings, there's no need for pretense. Am I right, JJ?"

"Sure, Rabbit. You want to do the rough stuff before dessert, I can swallow it."

"I bet you can," he now hissed, showing me that he was more than a little put out over my Friday afternoon escapade in his home. "Tell me," he went on, "did it even occur to you that in addition to your own rocks you might be jeopardizing someone else's health and well-being? Someone who has tried to treat you as a friend?"

"I assume you're referring to yourself," I offered quietly, hoping to calm him.

"You assume correctly," the Rabbit intoned in more of his native Sicilian accent than I was accustomed to hearing from him.

"What's the matter?" I asked. "You're not that afraid of Stanese to think—"

"I know how he thinks," the Rabbit interrupted, "and it's you who should be afraid."

"If it's any consolation," I said, "I am. One of his goons put the word to me in a restaurant yesterday. Over breakfast."

"You're kidding," Dot said, letting me know by the look on her face that she was not privy to all that was in the works even if the Rabbit was.

"Unfortunately not," I sighed.

"What are you then, a masochist?" the Rabbit pleaded.

"Well, I *do* try to make my living in the theater," I said in a feeble attempt at humor that went right by my host.

"Look, JJ," he now said almost with desperation in his voice, "I know Andee is beautiful, and young, and—"

"Tired of Matt Stanese," Dot interjected in a welcome show of support for the visitor's side.

At this, the Rabbit went silent, stood, cleared his plate from the table, and came back with more of the Peruvian white. He calmly brushed away the crumbs around him, laid out four lines, and sucked one right up with a rolled twenty-dollar bill which he then handed to me. "Please," he said, gesturing to the toot.

And I did my line. And so did Dot. And we all sat quietly until the buzz descended on the room.

Then the Rabbit leaned forward and with all his might blew the remaining line into oblivion with one quick explosion of breath. I was startled, as was Dot, and as the cloud of powder settled around us, the Rabbit leaned toward me over the table.

"Just like that," he said, "one minute you are feeling no pain, the next you are gone. Pfft."

And at the sound of this *pfft*, my stomach churned. "What's your interest, Rabbit?" I managed to ask. "I mean, we hardly know each other."

"I like you. Dot likes you. She wants to produce your play. I want to produce more movies."

And at last I understood. Stanese's arm reached somewhere into the coffer from which the Rabbit and his brother drew sustenance for their films. A line I had written in a letter to Lynn upon arrival in this fair city suddenly rang in my head. *Nothing like people involved in a project for selfish reasons. They're the ones you can count on.* I knew the Rabbit was telling me the truth.

I looked at Dot, who was looking down at the table-top, and then turned back to the Rabbit.

"Mind if I ask you one more question?"

"No," he mumbled.

"Why do they call you the Rabbit?"

He smiled.

"Because I am always one step ahead."

Shortly after that I was on my way. Dot walked me outside, my homemade, uneaten Rabbit cannoli in hand, and without saying a word she managed to let me know

119

that she comprehended the depth of my dilemma and felt not only for me, but for Andee. After all, she had been hearing Andee's side of the intrigue every morning at the studio, and I think even at that moment as she acknowledged the futility of my trying, she was pulling for me somehow. I thanked her for the meal, flicked some snow out of her hair, gave her a quick kiss, and walked off toward the corner to grab a cab.

"It's over," I said to myself, "there's even money at stake."

Back at Futterman's, I felt like Bogey just after he had kissed Ingrid Bergman off to the sky at the end of *Casablanca*. Only I hadn't played the scene yet, and I couldn't imagine how I would ever get to, given the circumstances. The cocaine had numbed me to the cold outside but ice had penetrated my heart. When I went for a Kleenex on my desk, I saw the note.

I haven't told you all that much about Futterman in my letters—I think because I'm afraid he's too good to be true. He and his wife have been ridiculously kind to me and almost without reason have decided that they have one of America's next great playwrights living under their roof for the winter. I mean, they know about the grants and the prizes and the productions out in the regional theaters. But he's talking Broadway, man. He's got fucking Dianne Aimsley taking my phone calls. And he hasn't so much as asked to see a single page since I sat down in his den. I have only to look him in the eye and nod, and he is content to leave me to the work.

But here I am, standing over the little round table that I call my desk, my heart emptying into my runny nose, and I see this note addressed in his handwriting, "To JJ." I know he's going out to California in the morning for some TV talk, so I figure it's a so-long and maybe even a few more spending bucks. But what's inside? A song of fear and trembling. Dame Maggie Steinfeld, who hereafter shall be known as the Cunt, has informed him by phone, while I was over at Dot's, that she suddenly has reservations about the project and the work I'm doing. Of course she hasn't seen any of it, but that isn't going to stop her from mouthing off behind my back.

So now Futterman is worried. He's off in his room, sound asleep, so I can't talk to him, but he's worried. He wants my reassurance that I'm leveling with him on my progress and he's a little pissed that something has happened between me and Maggie that he doesn't know about. He wants to hear from me while he's in California and have dinner when he gets back Thursday night.

Goddamn her, Deek. Do you know what happened between us? When Andee said she could see me Friday afternoon, I canceled a lunch the Cunt and I were supposed to have. We've already had ten of them and we're starting to repeat the restaurants we go to and absolutely nothing of importance was on the agenda, but she went berserk over my rearranging her day. Of course by now I've heard from Dot Penner that she may have another iron in the fire, that someone is offering her another play to direct up in New Haven, so I pen this in a note to Futterman and send it off to LA. But the damage is done. The spell has been broken. Doubt hangs in the air and it smells.

I open the pull-out and sink into it, staring bleary-eyed across the park at the million-dollar nests on Fifth Avenue and I'm still sweating from the Rabbit and his coke and the very idea that I've lost Andee when I'm just starting to believe I can have her, and within minutes I am dreaming. Except I'm not asleep. I'm up on that wire where cocaine leaves you when it's decided your body is no longer worthy of its high-minded attention. I'm abandoned by everything and everyone: my producer, my director, my California life, my New York love, even my drugs. The wire is all there is and I've put myself on it. Everyone else is down below looking up at me, maybe waiting for a fall. And I have to walk.

So I do.

And each step is a footprint of my soul. In one lies the crushed life of my play, its characters pleading with me to restore their voices. In another lies Andee, sleeping or drugged or dead. In the next Maggie and Stanese crouch laughing and reaching for my feet to trip me. Then there is Lynn with Futterman and his wife, all of them shaking their heads in regret.

But I'm making it, I'm moving forward. This is what progress is all about. Being up on the high wire and toeing your way across. So I lift my head high and breathe deep. And who do I see on the platform at the far end but my good buddy Deek. And I look at you the rest of the way, pal, and in the blink of an eye I am across. And happy. And out for the count.

When I awoke in the morning, it was to the sound of a buzz. At first I thought it was in my head, but then I realized someone was at the door. I wrapped myself in my comforter and stumbled out in the living room. When I opened the door, our favorite doorman stood there appraising me with absolute disgust. "Messenger for you," he grunted, and handed me an envelope. He didn't even wait to see if I was going to grease his palm; he just turned and walked back to the elevator. I looked into the front hall mirror and had to admit I did look like an ad for everything you wouldn't want your firstborn to grow up to be, but I smiled at my early A.M. coke eyes and stumbled back to the pull-out. It was only when I resumed the horizontal that I realized what I held in my clammy paw. It was a note from angel Andee O'Neill begging me to just tell her what to do and promising me she would do it.

I looked around the room for a moment. Light that

122

was beyond white was pouring in from the winter streets outside. I felt horribly vulnerable lying there naked, wrapped in a quilt. I was sweating and cold at the same time, as though inhabited by both the heat of Andee's note of desire and the ice of the Rabbit's warnings the night before. I reached over to the desk and grabbed my un-eaten cannoli and stuffed it into my mouth. It was tasty, if a bit dry (like everything else) from the steam heat. Then I grabbed a pencil and paper.

It was too early in the morning for breaking hearts, but I wrote Andee that maybe we should back off for now, at least until I saw what was going to happen with my play and with her and Stanese, etc. I told her that I wanted her in spite of the goons, that there was no forget-ting her, but that I didn't want to see my legs (or hers) broken. Let's give it some time, I said.

And the next thing I remember was the door buzzing again. I looked at my watch and it was just after 1:00. I assumed afternoon, as the light was still doing its best to burn holes in my retinas, and I again made my way out to the front hall. I swung the door open and the next thing I knew her ice cold satin cheeks were warming themselves by rubbing on my beard. Her eyes were as bright as the sun outside and her lips found mine with a desperate biting squeeze. She fought her way under the comforter and I felt the coldness of the city outside on her clothes. A sliver of snow fell on my bare feet.

"I gave it as much as I could," she said, staring beyond the sleep still there in my eyes.

"As much what?" I asked.

"Time."

And then she smiled her movie-star smile at me, white teeth framed by the silky darkness of all that long black hair. She had gotten the note I had just sent by messenger and this was her answer.

"Nobody's home?" she asked.

123

"Just the writer," I managed to answer as her cold hands found what they were looking for under the comforter.

"Great," she said. "I need my lines."

And then we were in the den. And her clothes were falling to the peg and groove. And the curve of her hip was silhouetted by the backwash of light as she approached me on the pull-out. She leaned down and her hair fell over my face and I looked up into that smile again. And we kissed hard. And grabbed at each other. Like airplane passengers when the realization sinks in that the plane is going in. Everything was hard, rough. We pulled and pushed at each other like street fighters. At one point somebody's lip got cut on a tooth. My cock got bit. Her thigh was scratched. We locked shoulders and pulled on hair. Her panties somehow ended up over the devil's horns on the likeness of Futterman across the room and we laughed. Later a belt tied our wrists together and we pretended we had only moments alone before an imaginary captor would return to separate us. Our arms stretched high above our heads in mock pain and our kisses grew soft. Eyelids heavy. Breathing deep. And all the time we rolled and pressed and turned and fell in unison. We embraced without arms. Pulled stomachs flat and together with straining thighs. Dreamt. Awakened. And dreamt again. Until it was over. And then starting again.

Later, in the shower, we both began to cry. Moments like this were meant to be savored, not abandoned. And yet, in order to arrive at the true bittersweet taste of our pain, I think it was necessary to believe that these might be our last seconds together. We held tight, soaping each other's backs, and I told her what had happened with Futterman. She told me of a hesitation in her agent's voice when she asked him about leaving the show to try movies. And then for a long time we just stood letting the water wash over us, as though we were dancers in a marathon, sound asleep on our feet.

But outside the shower something happened, Deek. A variation on the original mirror scene in your film. We were drying ourselves off, exchanging rubs and quiet smiles, when we locked eyes in the mirror on the back of the bathroom door. It got very still and I saw that what was happening was the same for both of us. She dropped her eyes and went up and down every square inch of my body as though with a magnifying glass. I did the same with hers. Then we dropped our towels and stood next to each other and stared at the reflection of our perfect fit. It wasn't the thrill of confronting an obsession or the excitement of an idea come to life. It was the chill of seeing what you have been looking for looking right back at you and knowing it was real.

"No way I'm letting go of this," she said, turning to me and taking my face in her hands.

A tiny droplet of water hung on one of her eyelashes like dew. I wrapped my arms around her, again melted into the silky moisture of her skin, and tried to send my tongue clear down her throat into her heart.

It was soon dark and she was gone and I was at my desk and the play was flowing through my pencil like it was the sword Excalibur. The lights started to come on in the windows of the Fifth Avenue penthouses across the park and Futterman's wife arrived home and told me she just didn't like Maggie Steinfeld. I turned down dinner, saying I didn't want to stop work, and I sat here in a trance for seven and a half hours as A train after A train rumbled through the ground below me. About 2:15 I realized I was in the final scene of the play and by quarter to three I had written LIGHTS TO BLACK.

The whole time, Deek, Andee's face hung there before me and with each word, with each speech, I tried

125

in vain to match its dark beauty. And unlike other frustrations in my life, this reaching for the impossible seemed to strengthen me, urge me on, rather than taunt me into weakness.

I know now I'm in love. I'm willing to risk everything for her.

Please advise on next move.

JJ

My Andee,

I want you to know, so we can be through with this silliness, that I have decided to forgive you. Time will heal our wounds but I would also like to offer my help.

I understand how this kind of thing can happen. Our lives have been exciting and fast since we came to New York. But let's not forget how we got here—by sharing, by wanting things together. You were nothing when I met you. Except in my eyes. It was me who saw what you could be. Me who grabbed you off the street up in Boston. Me who made it happen for you. And me who wanted to share in your happiness.

But as I said, I know this kind of thing can come along. You meet somebody from some faraway place and he looks good and talks a good line. Maybe he's even nice, and in the same business. You're a beautiful girl. Millions of men see your picture in a magazine or your face on the TV and want you. Which is fine. Let them. Every penny of their tiny desire puts a dollar in the bank for you. But, my Andee, you can't forget who you are and how you got to where you are.

I haven't asked for much from you, I don't think. Not in light of what I've done in return. Just your loyalty, that's all. A simple thing which life can be built around. Loyalty. Sticking together. Remembering. We're family, honey, and loyalty is what makes a family survive. It's in our blood. It makes us what we are.

127

All right, so you've had your fling. Maybe I haven't always paid enough attention to you, so you went out on the town and had a little fun. But let's call it a night, ok? Your Matty wants you back in his nice warm bed where he can hold you and take care of you and be sure you get what you want out of the world. You don't want to live hand-to-mouth with some writer. I checked—he's got nothing. In fact, he probably sees a meal ticket in you. Is that the kind of guy you think makes a woman happy? Personally, I don't see the attraction.

So come back. Please. Let's forget this happened and get back to what we had, what we still have, and always will. Nobody will ever love you the way I do. I worship you, my love. I know we've talked about this before, but I think it's time I asked you again. I'd like to get married. Maybe even buy a house out on the Island. We could have it all, Andee. We already do. Say yes. Say you'll do this for yourself. And for the one who adores you.

Your Matt

Mr. David Raskov
c/o The Wyndham Hotel
42 West 58th St.
New York, NY 10019

Dear David:

Glad *My Wife's Affair* struck the chord I thought it would in you. Here, for your return-trip perusal, are some answers, as it were, to your questions. (See enclosed copy of your memo if, by chance, any of them have slipped your mind.) By the number:

1) The film would cover a period of about six or eight months, from fall of one year until the following spring. Plenty of time for passions to die with the leaves, heat back up through sex in the snows and slush of winter, and bud with the May flowers for the rebirth of our couple's desire for each other in the spring.

2) Your hopes shall be fulfilled. As I understand this part, it is about sex with strangers. We will probably get to know something about at least one of each of our hero's lovers, but only as it can offer some humor and/or insight into our couple's past. (Segue to next question.)

3) Sex is the best way (in your assistant's humble opinion) to search out anyone's past. In some ways, it seems to me to be the perfect battleground between our past and present. In sex, the allure of past hopes confronts the disappointment of present realities. Or conversely, the overwhelming joy of good sex in the present does battle with the disappointments of failures in the past. In either

case, it is a natural way to get to know our couple through cuts from these winter lovers to key moments and events in their relationship (possibly even the same ones, seen from both sides) prior to the split. If the sex is good enough, I can guarantee that it will even sustain flashbacks if we want to use them (and I know you do) against all the little Baby Moguls' dictates.

4) I don't know if I can answer this question. I've fallen in love only once in my life. Perhaps reading the novel when it is completed will help to illuminate my thinking on the matter.

5) I would love it if the sex when our couple gets back together is absolutely delicious, the best of their lives, but for the time being, ditto Answer No. 4 above.

6) From my knowledge, sex was not a part of their problems really. They probably had their share of unspoken criticisms, etc., but I think their disappointment would be more the kind that comes with the inevitable familiarity stage in a relationship, where you realize that the person you are trying to get excited about is also the person who shits in your bathroom, snores on the pillow next to you, and dirties the dishes downstairs. It's the old mine field of wanting to be best friends with someone and then resenting the all-knowing almost brother/sister closeness that comes about as a result.

7) I guess for sex to be possible within a marriage, the trick would be to somehow avoid No. 6. (No pun intended.)

8) We *know* sex is possible without marriage. We know it very well. (No further comment, even though you're *not* kidding.)

9) See Question and Answer No. 4. (No offense, but you tend to repeat yourself when you drink, David.)

10) Ideally, both. If marriage is again *the* socially desirable thing, then a movie questioning its values is definitely going to upset people. But when our couple

130

gets back together, that will also obviously be reassuring. (And possibly in the ring of the cash-register sense of the word, as what we have here is the potential for massaging the current latent sociopolitical, econo-religious, wish-fulfillment fantasy of the ubiquitous, conspicuous, free-spending, credit-card-carrying saviors of the new/old American dream: the Young Urban Professionals. Amen.)

11) You know better than to ask me this question, David. Which would I rather do? I'd rather go into the theaters and take hostages until everyone in America re-membered the meaning of the word "disturb" and again stood up to demand its realization in films on the screens before them. (Think Coke would approve that?)

12) Who do I see as our heroes? Ideally? Henry and Stacey Winkler. Realistically? Some WASP gods like Meryl Streep and William Hurt.

13) Let's not get nasty about the little ones. Where would we be without their lack of memory and willing-ness to spend $4.75 for butter popcorn and a Coke? (Notice, I did say Coke.)

14) See the above, lucky No. 13, and prepare to commit ourselves orally to including a Pepsi challenge in the film only if Coke will guarantee to supply us with the Real Thing (and I mean *real*) free of charge in our offices and on the set for six months running as of the start of preproduction.

15) I see we're back to the serious stuff. . . . Yes, I think lust can be restored to a relationship if it has been misplaced for a minute. A minute and thirty seconds, no. But a minute? Definitely. (Especially if the free Real Thing for six months running is included in the attempt . . .)

16) You want to know if marriage is at all dependent on lust? Is the Pope Catholic?

17) Lust dependent on marriage? Do Catholics still listen to the Pope?

18) Would men and women answer the above differently? Am I envious of what you have in your pants?

19) I would say no, it doesn't influence who we select to write the film, assuming they don't have to drop their pants to get the job.

20) Your track record with marriage means you should disqualify yourself from life, not from the movies.

21) Things between me and JJ at the moment are: Chicago, Des Moines, Denver, Omaha, Santa Fe, and Bakersfield.

22) Where is JJ? Connect the dots.

23) I didn't say he was moving there. But for the sake of argument, let's say he does. Will I marry you? Will you publicly disavow your track record and morally, ethically, and legally disqualify yourself from attempting to produce my life?

24) The option to make more movies has, for the last two years and presumably the next ten, been, for you, just a phone call away. Why would living back in New York change anything? (Unless you're referring to the box office we would need to cover the cost of the calls.)

25) My job, much as you seem bent on minimizing its potential for improving your life, includes being in touch with working writers and knowing what will be coming from them before it comes. (Again, excuse the pun.) I happen to be familiar with this writer's work and, at the moment, in a position to know what will be forth. . . (Never mind, I just know.)

26) If you/we make him the right offer, he would be amenable. He might even be agreeable.

27) When do you like people to make deals with you—before or after?

28) Do you want to risk having to take a number and wait in line?

29) Steal the story? I thought you wanted to disavow your track record.

30) As for food fights, I would say that depends on whether Coke comes through with the Real Thing.

Look forward to discussing same and/or more of the above upon your return to the Land of Lotus.

Your obedient, ever-humble, and faithful (or faithless, if you prefer) servant,

Lynn Rodnick (yes, I was Jewish once) Towne

Tuesday, February 7

Mr. J. J. Towne
c/o Futterman
183 Central Park West
New York, NY 10023

Dear JJ,

Been a while, huh?

I just got back from having lunch with your producer over at the Polo Lounge. He called me at home this morning (I think, judging from the noise in the background, while he was sitting in his booth—you can always tell the New York people in there, no one else would be caught dead with a telephone at their table).

But I went and it was all right. Sort of. He seems a nice man and I agree with you that his heart is in the right place. He really wants the play to work out and I can tell he's grown very fond of you. I got the feeling there was almost a fatherly nice-Jewish-man-who-never-had-a-son quality about the way he talked of you. Heartwarming, to be sure, but a word to the wise, if I may. It could get a little sticky if the day arrives when you have to disagree with him over something. Partners in business can yell at each other without severing connections; fathers and sons can't. (Not that you're the yelling type anyway . . .)

So how's it going? Futterman says he's amazed by the hours you put in at your desk. I asked him if you're taking advantage of the city, too, and he said he sees you indulge occasionally but not with any extravagance. You know what they say, JJ, about all work and no play. . . I mean, unless I start hearing some stories of performing heads (i.e., the twins), I think I'm going to be disappointed in you. (Either that or I'm going to get paranoid about what I'm *not* hearing.)

Things are okay here. I've managed to find a story for David that we both agree may be the film we've been looking to make. Unfortunately, it isn't even written yet and the author doesn't know that I've mentioned what he told me about it to anyone, let alone a Hollywood producer. Can't tell you much either, except that I love the idea of it and it's the first time in two years that I've received a written memo from David more than half a paragraph long on anything.

Rudi and I are doing fine at home. Believe it or not, I've started feeling pretty comfortable being by myself. I'm even playing the piano again. And though it's been a couple of years (can that really be . . . ?), Rudi does the exact same thing she always did. She goes right under the bench, curls up in a little ball, and sighs in all the right places. When I was playing Schumann the other night, I thought the poor dog was going to cry. I don't care what anyone says, this dog understands music.

So, write me from the big city, huh? I'm staying busy, but not too busy to stop and savor your beautiful handwriting.

L & K,
Lynn

My music has returned! Out of the blue, I sat down the other night and poured through Band 1 of Brahms Klavier Werke, the Chopin Preludes (18 still kills me), the Schubert Phantasies, my Hindemith book from sixth grade (still don't play it like I did then), and the Schumann Scenes from Childhood. Hours went by and the piano, after letting me know at first that it had suffered from my neglect, began to come alive at my caress, as I did from the pure sensation of its touch. It was time travel. I made it clear back to Long Island, where I used to play by the open window in my house on summer nights when everyone else was out getting ice cream or whatever teenagers were supposed to be getting. I still remember the night my parents went into the city, leaving me alone in the house, when I took off all my clothes and played Beethoven until Stewie Kaplan whistled at me from somewhere out on the street. It was the first time I felt the sexuality of a piano, which is considerable, and which became a kind of stand-in for boys with me until I met Richie Morell and encountered his blue Stingray and his tight blue jeans and what was inside them.

But tonight it was just me and the piano again. In a house populated only by a dog who sighs. I took off my clothes again. And played again. And this time I consummated the intimacy that Stewie Kaplan's whistle shattered all those years ago. Now here I am, alone with my red notebook in a bed for two.

It was a strange day. Starting with answering David's questions on Deek's novel. He was drunk when he wrote

136

the memo to me, but I've never known him to let his guard down so, to let me see that beneath the bravado of his Harvard to Hollywood cynicism there lies, in fact, some open wounds. He's like so many people you meet out here who showed up after the 60's to make money from their fantasies instead of revolution and found that the business of fantasy was a far cry from their fantasy of business. He never quite managed to lose his distaste for the pursuit of money either, which the true Sammy Glicks can smell on him in a second here, and because of it he's been kept from the inner circle of power. The Baby Moguls like him—in fact, they share an honest affection for him—because he reminds them of what they might have been were it not for their decisions at some point to abandon their souls. They like to take David to lunch or dinner whenever they're feeling a bit of the old nostalgia for destruction. They like to just sit across a table from him and look. And see what becomes of hesitation. What becomes of he who tries to keep one foot outside the door, who tries to keep his soul only at arm's length instead of locking it in the trunk of the Jag. They get their fill by stuffing him full of food at Ma Maison and when they're done—when the pity wells up in their gut, that is—they pay him for the reassurance he has provided them with, for erasing the guilt they still harbor over abandoning all sense of commitment. They give him a development deal or something. Just enough to keep him in money so he'll stay around. And stay the same. As long as he doesn't make any movies, nobody loses anything. Very cozy, this relationship. It's productive without risk. Enlightening without threat. Rewarding with a minimum of cash flow. What could be more Hollywood? You use someone and they're grateful for it. Everything moves forward while everything stays the same.

Then the lunch with Futterman over at the Beverly Hills Hotel, pink palace of egomania. Suits jockeying for the preeminent corner table. All the latest variations in lapels. The right—or rightest—Rolex. And the ever-present Mercedes ladies arguing which is better, the cracked crab or the baby shrimp.

Futterman apparently has "his" table when he is out here (a remnant from the past?), and Bernice Philbin calls him by his first name. I'm impressed, I guess. Except that he seems like just another schmuck to me, if a little less prone to the vicious. We talk and he refers to JJ in a patronizingly possessory way, as though this time that he's spending in New York is a pilgrimage made possible by a grant from the Peter Futterman foundation, like JJ is some lost soul from the sticks who has been brought to the city by Big Daddy, The Patron Saint of the Hopelessly Undiscovered. Christ, he's given JJ a hundred bucks twice, most of his dinners, and a pull-out bed in a room that doesn't have a door. Oh, and he optioned the play for six months for $500. I don't mean to sound ungrateful—it is Central Park West and all—but JJ sometimes plays the modesty bit to excess. In my opinion, he should be getting all his expenses and a hotel room of his own choosing. He hasn't been on Broadway before, that's for sure, but he is, as he himself likes to point out, one of the better known of the unknown playwrights in this country. And this trip is costing *him* (i.e., us) money.

JJ reminds me, however, that this is the theater, not the movies, and I chide myself for my Hollywood appetites in the face of distinguished New York purity. Except that Futterman lets slip that he's out here to put the touch on a deal to make a TV movie in China. Very big stuff for TV, he tells me, the first of its kind if he pulls it off. And then he gets all self-conscious, as though he suddenly remembers who I am in this succession of LA faces across "his" table and into "his" booth. And I'm probably going to pick up the phone and tell this to his little playwright who is working his ass off in hopes that his play might appear on Broadway come fall when in reality his producer is hoping to be scarfing down Peking duck under the October leaves—in Peking! Or, as Mr. New York says, "Bee-jing."

I order the most expensive thing on the menu and talk about every production of every play JJ has ever written, starting with the one-act that won him the Hopwood Prize as an undergraduate at Michigan and moving through the Yale Drama School years, the summer up at the O'Neill, the regional theater productions all over the country, and his cult status as playwright-in-exile in Southern California. I surprise even myself at the depth of my presentation, as if I'm doing a summation before a jury or a grant request for the Rockefeller family (which JJ has also been the humble recipient of).

Futterman doesn't know quite what to make of it either. He listens, he nods, he smiles. But I can see he is thinking TV. All the way. That's what he's here for and that's what's in his blood. None of this JJ stuff now, please.

TV people get this look in their eyes. I've seen it. It's kind of a cathode ray tube glow. Even people in the studios fear it. Because with it come all these numbers and you have to know what they mean and unless you make the right calls to the right people at 8 AM (New York time) your numbers aren't going to be the right ones and you're not going to be part of the club. Except that you don't want to be part of the club. You've hated television since your parents forced you to watch Sid Caesar and Imogene Coca in 1956 and pretend it was something you found funny. You have nightmares of ugly black and white RCA TV sets with overheated vacuum tubes inside them coming at you in the bed of your childhood. You've wanted to smash TVs all your life, even when they brought pictures of Vietnam and your head being smashed in Chicago, circa 1968, into the same living room that your parents now sat in in a certifiable state of shock. TV is the devil's work, to your way of thinking. Fuck TV, and fuck anyone who has ever had anything to do with it.

But you say, "Thanks for the lunch, Mr. Futterman. It was wonderful to meet you, and give JJ a hug."

And you get up and shake hands. And nod to a friend at a table across the room. And offer Bernice Philbin a sweet see-you-next-time smile on your way out the door. And out in the driveway you hand the cute blond boy in his red waist jacket the ticket for your car. And two dollars when he drives it the twenty feet over to you. And once inside, you turn on the radio and listen to a rock and roll group called The Police as you drive into Coldwater Canyon toward your piano and dog at home. And you think of your husband long gone and too far away as you call your lover on the phone.

Welcome to your life. It is "The 80's" and you are a woman of independent means.

Thursday, February 9

Mr. J. J. Towne
c/o Futterman
183 Central Park West
New York, NY 10023

Hey, J—

Loved your last two letters. Hope you won't mind if I lift
them right into my book. (You're not bad with prose
yourself, you know . . .)

As I write this, you're probably having your reconciliation meal with Futterman. I trust everything is straight,
especially since your marathon Monday night put you
over the top with the rewrite. Personally, I love when that
kind of rush grabs on to me and drives me right through to
the end of something as though time didn't exist. After
reading your letter describing how Andee's face did it for
you, I decided I should check her out for myself. I don't
know why I didn't think of it sooner either. It was just a
question of setting the old VCR. (You'll forgive me for not
abandoning the novel at noon, even for an hour. . . .)

So I set the machine, I finish my day at the desk, I
pour myself a good stiff triple sec straight, and I flip on
your fave soap and mine, *Down by the River*, via TDK
time delay. Mind you, I'm a little blitzed—good day and
good drink, characters and real life spinning at the same
time before me—so at the sound of the organ I start to
laugh. I think to myself, JJ's lost it, he's gone over the
edge this time, he can't really be taking anything to do
with this seriously. But then she appears before me in the
first scene of the show, resplendent, as they say, in lace

teddy, one strap dangling, then falling, from what everyone knows is this man's main weakness in the world, a beautiful silky shoulder which is promptly dusted by a cascade of free-floating blackness that looks like a commercial for what hair is supposed to be. And I'm gone. Yes, I'm still laughing, but now at my best buddy's good fortune, and at God for his charming sense of humor in the way he distributes what, for lack of a better word, we, the feeble, call beauty. Yes, this is a face one could live for. And I'm not totally unaware of the body beneath it either. Forgive me for doubting you, JJ. The threat of death wouldn't keep me from this woman either.

So, I guess it's decision time, huh? Especially since you're through with the play (at least for now) and she seems to feel she's through with the godfather. The way I see it, you probably can't stay in New York, though, and you probably can't come here. How's your family in Chicago these days?

Seriously, JJ, what do you think you want to do? Can you really picture yourself in the world without Lynn? My interest is obviously for your welfare, but I confess there's more to it than just that. You know, it doesn't surprise me anymore when we end up dancing around the same themes in our work, but I can't help but be amazed when our lives seem to run parallel courses even when we're separated by continents. I've said at times that you are my alter ego, but occasionally it feels more like twins or something, where one knows what the other is up to before making or getting the long-distance call that will confirm that the knowledge is true.

Yeah, I'm involved in something like this right now too. I haven't told you about it because I didn't want you to confuse it with what's happening to you. You write that all this reminds you of Ibsen, but if it has to be one of those dark Swedes, I'll take Strindberg. Midnight passions, uncontrollable impulses—all leading to ruination. Or the savior, depending on your point of view.

In my book, I'm trying to decide which. It's funny how we try to solve the riddles of our lives by turning them into fiction, isn't it? I mean, here you are talking of the drama of letters in your life right now and over the years you've been refining this delivery of offstage news into the dramatic technique that drives your plays. And for me, in my books, I've been trying for a long time to draw a self-portrait by painting scenes just at the edge of my frame of reference, scenes that advance my narrative by working around the action instead of through it, and that's a pretty fair description of what's going on these days under my own roof, too. Like the way Hemingway used to say that what is important to a story is what is left out, I think we both like our faces to emerge from the background by way of what we choose not to reveal. It's a subtle effect, but if it works, our audience intuits the lines of our faces by the way we arrange their perception of our stories instead of by our pulling them through the mud of reality like the blind leading the blind. The irony, of course, is that we both *are* blind right now with regard to how to live our lives.

I've been thinking a lot about what you said about triangles. I think there's something there that helps me understand it all, because there's no doubt that I, too, am, and always have been, pulled by their magic.

I'm a single man sleeping with a married woman, JJ, and writing a book about a separated married couple who sleep their way back together. You're a married man, separated from your wife, sleeping with a single woman, and writing a play about a woman who walks away from what she thinks of as the sexlessness of married life. Both of our stories are based on real-life occurrences. And we're writing each other letters about those stories and about our real lives. I'm also using the real-life you for a

143

certain inspiration in my fiction. And you're using what I learn from my fiction to help yourself straighten out your real life. Is it any wonder that we see triangles when we pause to come up for air?

People casually call these things love triangles, just like they casually say that in matters of the heart, opposites attract. I think it would be more accurate to say that we are attracted not to our opposite, but to the opposite of the one whom we once thought would be our all. I think we sit uncomfortably above our desire like the apex on some living obtuse triangle. When you're in love, it's always me, him/her, and something else. This, that, and another. What we want, what we don't want, and what we have. There is, sitting on our shoulders, the good angel, the bad angel, and our head. And beneath this little triangle of grey matter is still another, one which we feel but cannot name, one that is embodied in the human heart itself, pulsating, forever changing in shape, and yet forever remaining the same: a living, beating triangle. And if the heart itself is a triangle, then maybe so is love. And the lives of those in love. And those they are in love with.

I'm going to stop here because I get the feeling I'm starting to sound like what I am at the moment—a drunk. Why do you suppose we get sad in this life when we describe ourselves as we really are? It was my impression back at Yale that such an accomplishment would ring the bells of joy. Always.

Deek

P.S. Eat your breakfast at home until this thing with Andee and Stanese is settled, huh?

PETER FUTTERMAN

Friday, February 10

JJ—

I wanted to let you know how terrific and grateful I feel this morning to have the play in hand. As I said last night over dinner, I just didn't expect it this soon, in spite of the long hours I've seen you putting in. You couldn't have welcomed me back home with a finer gift.

As you see, I've left you a small token of my appreciation for your diligence. Please have yourself a weekend on the town or something. You deserve to celebrate!

We'll deal with Maggie and the rest once I've read the script.

Again, my thanks for your hard work. And congratulations!

Fondly,
Peter

THE PLAZA

Friday, February 10

Miss Andee O'Neill
c/o "Down by the River"
Warwick Studios
5460 Seventh Ave.
New York, NY 10020

Andee—

Gave the play to Futterman last night and he gave us
Room 1402 here for the weekend. They've got toothbrushes
in the medicine cabinet and doormen downstairs to protect us. I'm waiting for you.

Love,
JJ

THE PLAZA

Friday, February 10

Miss Dot Penner
c/o "Down by the River"
Warwick Studios
5460 Seventh Ave.
New York, NY 10020

Dear Dot,

Enclosed please find your copy of the play. I gave it to Futterman last night and saw that he messengered one down to Maggie this morning. Didn't want you to feel left out.

As you probably know, I will be incommunicado for the weekend. Please don't let your old man know where.

Thanks. Call us when you've read it.

JJ

DOWN BY THE RIVER

Friday, February 10

Mr. Matt Stanese
121 Chambers St.
New York, NY 10013

Dear Matt,

I'm sorry for my silence since you left me your note. I do want to answer. I just need some time to think. I'm so confused. I know what you're saying about the loyalty. Believe me, I don't go through a single day without remembering where I'd be without you. It's just, we've come a long way since Boston. You said so yourself. We're both different now—it isn't just me. And loyalty also means being true to yourself.

I'm going to spend the weekend alone and try to sort things out. Okay? Don't worry about me. It's just for the weekend. I'll be fine. And so will you. Maybe we both could use the time to think.

I'll see you Sunday. Maybe you'll take me to dinner at The Charcuterie? Our table? So we can talk?

Love,
Andee

THE PARADOX OF ONE

It is Friday night. The lights are out. And the sounds of the world fade outside the window. In the dark, the two lovers sigh as their hands search the privacy of each other's softnesses. Where is love and marriage and the absolutes of morals in such a moment? Compared to the danger of the fingers' dance in this darkness, what does safety have to offer? At least half of my pleasure comes from the strangeness of his touch, not knowing what he will reach for next. At least half of his comes of not knowing what his reach will find. If I love someone purely, their desire seems to die. If I lie my way to this darkness, I almost have to shy away from the fire. I am the baby who sticks tongue into flame, and the old mannequin who wants for any sensation, even pain. I love the warmth of the heavy wrap on a cold winter's night. And the chill of the abandoned waif in the rain. I want my lover to lie heavy on me until I can't even breathe. And I want freedom, the cool push on my back of a breeze. I want everything taken care of for me, so I don't even have to speak. And I want to yell at every fuck who did me wrong until all bow humbly at my feet. I want one cock in hand and two in the bush. And I want the celibacy of the religious, to take my pleasure from prayer and sweetness and books. If love conquers all, then I want to lie down in defeat. And yet I want to dance on my lovers' graves, left behind to laugh and to weep. When I feel his come inside me, I could be anyone, anytime, anyplace, who ever felt the heat of a thousand wasted lives draining slowly from inside them. And yet it is only me, so accustomed to this liberated waste that I have learned to draw my pleasure from it. What is betrayal—staying or going? Is it physical? Can you touch it? Taste it? Smell it? Or is it spiritual? Something that eats away at you from within, leaving you one day with a hole where you once had a heart. I always wanted to be at one with someone until I finally was and found that with one you have no company. Now I am left to lie in a strange room in the dark in order to get back to two. And of course, having done this, I again long for one. But which one? The one in whom the danger of unfamiliarity will live, at least for a while? Or the one whose insides I know like the back of my hand? And what of the back of my hand? I looked down at it the other night as it danced across 88 ivory keys giving voice to ten minor chord preludes, and the sight of my own skin terrified me. For the first time in my life, my hand looked old. Or older than I wanted. But I get ahead of myself. It is, as I said, a Friday in the dark. And this is Sunday talk. Tonight I am a spoon in a room with a lover. My breasts are pushing through his shoulder blades. My hips cradle his baby's ass. And in my hands rest his heart and his breath and his sighs. I roll him over on top of me. I pretend I am not there. I am a man lying flat on my back alone and I have a desperate desire for soft. Naturally this makes me grow hard. And naturally in my disappointment I smile. My grip surrounds the paradox. In the darkness, my fingers search out the truth. And its opposite. As the man above laughs, the paradox below cries. Truth comes in darkness. Well before the dawn. I am a witness to it. And also its pawn.

PETER FUTTERMAN

Saturday, 2/11

Miss Dot Penner
160 West End Ave., No. 2
New York, NY 10024

Dear Dot:

Enclosed please find the new draft of JJ Towne's play, *The Woman Asleep on the Library Bench,* which he delivered to me upon my return from California Thursday evening.

I have read it and so has Maggie Steinfeld and I would like to ask that you do the same and join us tomorrow for brunch at my apartment around 11:00, when we intend to discuss it.

It is my understanding, Dot, that although we have not been in touch while JJ has been working, you still maintain an interest in involving yourself in the play's production. If this is so, then I hope you'll join Maggie and me tomorrow.

Best regards,
Peter

PETER FUTTERMAN

notes: 2/11
re: *The Woman Asleep on the Library Bench* rewrite

1- the play now has a better sense of time about it; the descent of this woman is therefore more focused

2- some good writing in the new lines (individually); feels more like New York (as it should)

3- structure still a problem, too many scenes, still don't like each one titled, too episodic, filmlike

4- major questions still remain as to whether the course C. chooses to follow is believable, i.e., would a woman in this day and age who felt stifled in a marriage be capable of preferring life on a park bench to her home?; why doesn't she just get a place of her own?; or tell her husband to?; after all, she has a job, doesn't she? and credit cards?; what actually causes her to end up on the bench?; why does she stay there?

5- the rape: what does it say?, Maggie S. insists that one cannot have a rape in a play that is not a play about rape; JJ's point is that the rape actually happened, that this is a true story; but what is that story saying—that a woman who leaves a marriage for the sake of her sexuality is asking to be raped?; and do we want to be associated with such a story even if it is true?

6- Regardless, the play does not succeed by my standards of what a play is supposed to do; there is no sense of clarity about beginning, middle, and end; plot twists do not come out of the unexpected and pique the curiosity with surprises; likewise with lines and character motivation; hopes do not rise and fall with a true

152

sense of emotion; and there is no heart-wrenching climax and dénouement; a Broadway audience must either laugh or cry; thinking alone will not make for a run; in short this is still only an outline for a play at best.

SUM:

I like JJ Towne and believe he has done his best to incorporate the suggestions we all made to him before he started this draft, but clearly he has not accomplished what we all hoped for. The demands of the commercial theater are very different from the small art houses this playwright has spent most of his career working in. As Dianne Aimsley said to him upon their introduction, "The big arenas have their own rules, honey, and if you decide you want to play them, you'd best pay attention." Maggie suggests that perhaps JJ would be more comfortable writing for films with his staccato scene rhythms. I don't think this is the case, as JJ has insisted all along that if his sense of structure in this play is anything, it is Brechtian epic theater. He likes to develop his characters' histories in Brecht's oblique way of implying events and their ramifications at a distance of one step removed. But as Maggie says to that, who ever made a dime off of Brecht? I am aware that something has happened between JJ and Maggie personally that has clouded their professional interaction, and yet I find myself agreeing with much of what she says even when I am inclined to take JJ's side emotionally. There must be more than a missed lunch date between them, but I am at a loss to say what. Perhaps Maggie is indeed looking for a way out of the commitment, as JJ says. In either case, it does not bode well for any future collaboration. I have messengered the script to Dot Penner to get a third reaction in hopes that a more noninvolved party may shed some light on the dispute. My inclination at this point, however, is to pass on the play, unless the playwright is willing to proceed with extensive revisions on his own (i.e., during China).

THE PLAZA

Sunday, February 12

JJ, my love,

As I sit here watching you sleep, I can't help but think that as of this moment my life has forever changed. I think I knew it when I wrote you from the last hotel room I was in. But out there in California, I have to admit, I wondered if the sun and the breeze and all the garden smells were making me feel as if I had died and gone to heaven, even though I felt it was just being in love. Now the sky outside is gray, the park down below is barren, the streets are filled with the ugly frozen dirt of winter, and I know for sure that the warmth in my heart is because of you.

I look at you lying there and my eyes drink in your beauty. Your wavy hair and light brown eyes, your gymnast's shoulders and tennis player's thighs. Your long back and sweet little boy's behind. And your hands, which though I don't know, I guess are your dad's surgeon hands—I've never seen or felt the touch of such hands in my life. And your skin, so thick and smooth. And your cock which I so adore, I could kiss and suck and hold it against my heart for the rest of my life except for when it's inside me making me think I'm going to die, which I would gladly do if you would come with me and we could come together like that for all eternity.

JJ, I love you. And I've decided I'm going to do whatever I have to do to be with you. You've finished your play, which I know everybody's going to adore. You wrote it out of our happiness, so its future is going to be ours. You're going to be on Broadway and Dianne Aimsley

155

is going to thank God for discovering you when she accepts her Tony. Futterman is going to laugh all the way to the bank for taking a chance on you. And even Maggie Steinfeld is going to bare her crooked teeth to the world in joy for having had the honor of working with you. And when you run up there in your tux looking like Adonis, you're going to be mine and there's going to be a huge red lipstick mouth on your cheek to prove it. And we're going to run out of there and get married and go wherever you want to go for the rest of our lives because I know now that all I need is your voice in my ear to be happy forever.

Did I ever tell you how I love your voice? Just the sound of it makes me smile. I sometimes take out the matchbook you wrote that note to me on at Melon's that night and listen over and over in my mind to our first hello. I said hello to my future that night, JJ. I knew it then as I know it now—in my heart. And it's funny to me, too, because I always knew it would come to me that way, on the sound of a voice. Want to know a secret of mine? When I was a girl back up in Boston and my dad would come in my room in the middle of the night the way I told you, I used to hold this silly mountain lion doll afterward and it would talk to me and tell me not to worry, that no matter what, everything was somehow going to be all right. It had the sweetest voice and it would sing me back to sleep. And I would hold it close to me so my dad wouldn't hear and take it away. I've never told this to anyone, but I still have it. Sometimes I hold it after I've been with Matt. And you know what? When you leaned close to me that night at Melon's I thought I was drunk or going crazy because your voice was its voice. That's why I looked so embarrassed and smiled at you the way I did. It scared me, but I knew on the spot that all the time that voice had been in my ear for a reason. So it's real after all, I thought. It belongs to this cute guy from California. I have to know who he is.

So now I know and I love you, JJ. I've come a long way from those nights up in Boston to this room in The Plaza hotel, but finally I'm here, where I can listen to the voice for real. I can hear it now, even while you sleep. I can hear it in the sweet notes you write me. And in the love you make to me. And I want to hear it forever. Until the day I die. Because then I'll know that everything is going to be fine forever. The voice belongs to my love. Just like I always thought.

In this room today, with New York City outside my window, I, Andee O'Neill, did find my voice and true love in JJ Towne.

yours forever, JJ
Andee

PETER FUTTERMAN

Sunday, 2/12

Dear JJ,

I've read your play, as has Maggie Steinfeld, and while we both feel that you've made substantial progress toward a viable commercial script, I'm afraid I must also tell you that I don't feel satisfied that we can proceed to production on the basis of this rewrite. Susie and I have a dinner engagement tonight, so I'm sorry I can't go over it with you immediately, but I want you to know /////—

PETER FUTTERMAN

Sunday, 2/12

Dear JJ,

I've read your play, as has Maggie Steinfeld, and while we both feel that you've made substantial progress toward a viable commercial script, we're still undecided as to whether we should go right into a production of the play here in New York or perhaps try it out of town first. Susie and I have a dinner engagement tonight, so unfortunately I cannot go over the details of our thinking with you immediately, but rest assured that I will do so at the first available /////—

PETER FUTTERMAN

Dear JJ,

I've read your play, as has Maggie Steinfeld, and while we both feel that you've made substantial progress toward a viable commercial script, neither of us is certain that we would stand a good chance of keeping Dianne Aimsley on the project by showing her this version of the play. As you know, she was looking for a role at this time that would /////—

PETER FUTTERMAN

Sunday, 2/12

Dear JJ,

I've read your play, as has Maggie Steinfeld, and while we both felt that you had made substantial progress toward a viable commercial script, we were not certain that all our doubts and questions about the original version had been addressed satisfactorily. So we decided to show this draft to Dot Penner and see what her reaction would be as well. Unfortunately this did not really help matters, as she feels that the original was stronger by far. So we are at a temporary standstill, as it were.

Susie and I have a dinner engagement tonight, but perhaps when we get home you and I can talk a bit. I'd like to go over things alone with you before bringing Maggie and Dot back into the situation, because I honestly feel that whatever direction we now go in, neither of them will be involved.

Please don't be too discouraged, JJ. I continue to believe in you as a writer and I feel strongly that this play can somehow be brought to its potential. As you know, the road to a commercial production is inevitably lined with potholes, and perhaps we will simply have to be more patient with this play's journey through the streets of New York.

I hope you enjoyed your weekend. You should feel proud of your accomplishment and know that I am aware of how hard you have worked on your play. It will happen somehow, JJ. I firmly believe that.

Sincerely,
Peter

Sunday, February 12

Miss Dot Penner
160 West End Ave., No. 2
New York, NY 10024

Dear Dot,

I just got home from Futterman's and tried to call you, but your service says you're already gone for the evening. Since I have to leave tonight for New Haven, I thought I'd drop you a quick note before I pack.

I have to thank you one more time for telling me what was going on in the background with our boy, the playwright. I guess people from California just don't have it in them to dedicate themselves to anything (except maybe hedonism). What did he think—that there's nothing more to getting a Broadway play on than writing it? That since there's no sun here in the winter that he had to spend his free time lying around in bed with people's girlfriends? His sex life is really none of my business, but I committed to this project and gave it my all for the better part of this winter. I don't think it was too much to ask that he do the same. Maybe that's the way they do things out on the coast (no wonder movies are so deep these days), but he should have realized that he was running with the big boys here and that putting himself in danger was putting the project in danger. Opportunity knocks but once in this city, if at all. Obviously he slept right through his chance.

Funny thing is, this draft of the play isn't that bad.

I've gone into production with a lot worse. So maybe by the time I get through up in New Haven and China is over, Futterman will realize that and listen if I tell him I've changed my mind about it. Your saying that you felt the first version was still stronger was actually the perfect thing to confuse him into inaction at the moment, so I'm grateful. This way I may get to have my cake and eat it too. That is, if lover boy isn't deep-sixed by Rabbit's friend by then. (God, when I think of the coincidence of Rabbit knowing of JJ's problems *and* hearing about Futterman's China movie, it really scares me. I could have said no to this thing in New Haven and ended up 0 for 2 . . .)

Anyway, don't worry, you played Futterman just right and he told me after you left that he really respected you for leveling with him on the play. I'm sure that if I revive the thing over the summer, he'll still be glad to have you along on it.

I'll call you from Connecticut, but take care of yourself and give those alert little Rabbit ears a kiss from me. As for Mr. Los Angeles, I'm going to leave him up in the air so that when I call him (or should I say if I call him) in August, he'll be appropriately grateful. Maybe you could have Rabbit do his best to keep him alive at least until then anyway.

Love, love
Maggie

Sunday, February 12

Mr. Peter Futterman
183 Central Park West
New York, NY 10023

Dear Peter:

I wanted to thank you again for your honesty today regarding Towne's play. Your insight into its workings and deficiencies was truly a lesson for me in the secrets of Broadway. I suppose it just goes to show that my instincts about you being the kind of producer I always thought I wanted to work with are wonderfully accurate, but I wanted you to know, nevertheless, how grateful I am to learn from a master such as yourself.

Of course, I feel for the playwright, but I'm sure you will handle him with all delicacy and restraint. And who knows—he might learn from the experience as well and come back to us with the play rewritten as it should be.

As for Dot Penner, well, I had heard she was good with scripts in the early stages, and perhaps for off-Broadway things like she's been involved with, this is true. But she was obviously in over her head on this one. I guess soap operas and Broadway just don't mix. . . My apologies for bringing her in in the first place.

I'll be away for a few days trying to regroup. I have to admit that my expectations were so high for this project that it's going to take some adjusting on my part to get over it and move on to something else. But feel free to call if anything comes up. I'll be getting my messages and of course would be at your disposal.

Again, Peter, thanks. I look forward to our working together the day the elements fall in place the way we both would like them to. Please give my best to Dianne Aimsley as well, and thank her for the time she gave.

Sincerely,
Maggie

Mr. Richard Case
27 Saltair Road
Malibu, CA 90233

Dear Deek,

Your letter of last Thursday was just slipped to me by an unseen hand. Unseen because my eyes are still spinning. Have been since about 7:00 last night. I've read the treatise on triangles 33 1/3 times and no matter how much sense it makes, I am still in an irreversible funk. Fucked up is what I am. Spatially, temporally, and certifiably (i.e., really) fucked up . . .

    Here's the jam.

    I finish the play, as I told you, last Monday night. I score a G of coca (as in un-cola) and spend the better part of three days at the keyboard of Futterman's trusty brown IBM putting it in print. I come up for pizza only once in there that I can remember. My eyes, ears, nose, and throat, not to mention my fingers, legs, toes, and back, ache with a capital A for the effort, but before me sits in a brand spanking new saucy red cover the newest draft of six weeks of hyper-drive intra-sexual investigation, otherwise known as the rewrite of my play. And I am happy. It is 3:00 Thursday afternoon, one hour and twelve minutes before the Man's Regent Air space limo is due to land at Newark from Lotusland. The plan is for him to proceed with business and return home around 6:00, at which time we will consume mass quantities in a surprise celebration of our Broadway future. I have told two humans of my progress: the honorable Deek the Drunk (i.e., you), and the Angel Andee O'Neill. Not even Her Highness, the Poetaster of Parched Pussy, Directrix Extraordinaire, Ms. Maggie "the Cunt" Steinfeld, knows I have finished, let alone typed, this monster. And this makes me smile. We've talked about this, Deek, the one truly happy moment you have as a writer, when you've decided something is finally done, when it sits there on the desk looking like a newborn child, all innocent and giggling, free of criticism, unsuspecting and strong, and you can look at it and take a deep breath and feel a sense of true accomplishment even though you know it will eventually be shredded like so much shit when it hits the fan of the world's perception. So you drink in the glory, right? Which is what I did before dropping trow, yanking open the pull-out, setting my alarm, and coasting into the ozone for the better part of three hours.

The next thing I know, I'm dreaming of the A train down below and it's blowing a whistle as it rumbles by my bed every other minute and I can't escape the damn sound, so I open my eyes to look for a way out of the station and I realize where I am and that the whistle is in my bedroom and, in fact, attached to me. It's my diver's watch beeping like a tiny harbinger of doom on my own damn wrist. I punch it off, sit up as best I can, and see my wasted face all distorted in the blank Sony at the foot of the bed. I briefly imagine myself on the *Today* show chatting about my play with Jane Pauley while sitting next to Dianne Aimsley and then I slide into the bathroom for a groan-in-the-pipes New York shower.

By the time Futterman rolls in around 7:15, I am plastered. I had figured one small G&T would help me make my presentation of the play to him truly artful, but his delay has caused me to refill the glass one too many times. He strolls in, sets down his Louis Vuitton, and stares at me with something approaching horror. I can think of no way to speak, so I simply extend my hand

167

with my offering in red. He looks at it, takes it from me, opens it, realizes that against all hope it is indeed the play, and he smiles the kindest long-distance smile I think I've ever had the pleasure of experiencing while standing right in front of someone. We're buddies again. Whatever darkness there was before he left is forgotten. We're going to go out for dinner, stuff ourselves, and collapse in glee for the night. Which we proceed to do. With gusto.

When I wake up Friday morning, he's left me a note of thanks and fifty bucks with instructions to do the town on him for the weekend. Of course, I know that this and a credit card will buy me a cup of coffee in this city, but I am grateful and I proceed immediately to the nearest luxury palace, The Plaza, where I check in under a phony name with only my duck bag and sunglasses, giving your address, and I quickly summon the Angel Andee to room 1402 and my side. She's told Don Corleone that she needs to be alone for the weekend to think on his recent proposal of, yes, marriage, and she arrives with her neon smile in full arc and proceeds to bathe me with glorious kisses and promises of love. For the next thirty hours I keep awakening to such sights as her long mane of black hair lightly feather-dusting my dancing dick while she kneels smiling above me, a Puerto Rican from room service uncorking bottles of iced champagne and dipping them into silver buckets with a wicked grin in his eyes, my own face descending to a crystal hand mirror lined with fine brownish-white toot, and Andee's dark gentle form sinking into a mineral bath she has drawn for us in our candlelit peach marble bathroom. Somewhere in the midst of it all, I guess I pass out for good with the taste of her breath and lips in my lungs, and when I wake I find the sweetest note she's written me to date resting on her pillow. In it she says she's found in my voice a real-life version of a voice that she's carried within herself from childhood and that she wants me whispering sweet lovings in her ear with it now and forever. I sit up and examine what appears to be a scene of glorious debauchery overlooking Central Park, and then fall back on my pillow to savor every delicious lick that I can remember.

But as sure as the sun rises, it also falls. And I am back on the icy streets of the concrete isle heading up CPW to Futterman's den past frozen Sunday faces in the dark. When I arrive, the place is filled with cigarette smoke but is dead silent. I look in a couple of ashtrays and see some crushed Gauloises. Dame Hindquarters Steinfeld has been here, wafting the place with her idea of French intellectual stench. I walk through the long hallways past the six-foot Russian painting and Ben Shahn lithos and turn into the dining room. Five (yes, five) small round tables sit ominously empty in front of a wall of collected antique china plates. Another Gauloise butt though. This one sopping up coffee in one of Futterman's best Japanese porcelain teacups which has been carelessly abandoned on an oak side table and is forming a nasty ring in the untreated wood.

I turn and retreat from this depressing emptiness into my room. I'm taking off my jacket and unwinding my scarf when I see the note. It's sitting propped against my notebook over on the round table-desk. Foreseeing disaster for some reason (experience maybe?), I move to the envelope like Indiana Jones in the temple of doom, waiting for the ax to fall, the arrows to fling themselves from hidden crevices into my heart. I pick it up. I tear open the envelope, which is sealed. And there it is. They hate the play. Futterman, the Cunt, even Dot Penner. It's over. Futterman tries to say something about the future, that it will still happen for me, but it's horseshit. He knows it; I know it. It's over.

I float over to the IBM by the window, look down at it like it has betrayed me, like this cannot be happening. But it is. And it isn't the typewriter that has failed; it's me.

169

One more time I've made it all the way to the gate, the door has been opened, the announcements made, and I've been unable to walk on through. I remember, against my own will, all the other times this has happened. The play out in Minneapolis that couldn't lose. Until it did. The ones up in New Haven which propelled actors into New York and money and fame and yet somehow left me on Chapel Street without cab fare. The one out in Seattle which was talked about as though it heralded the second coming, and then found itself, along with me, going. I was in Chicago just before the theater that was doing my play there hit the map. I was in Louisville and San Diego and Denver and D.C., either a little early or a little late with plays that were either a little dry or a tad short of great. And I was in New York, right here in Futterman's den, close enough to Broadway to feel the heat. There was, as always, the great promise. It's been there, I can testify, since I was born. It's like that line in *Somebody Up There Likes Me*—I could be sued in court for breach of promise, I've showed it so many goddamn times and then come up short.

So I look around me. I remember the night I arrived here, when the room made me sick. And the afternoon when I met Maggie and we sat on the floor, got stoned, and I stared at her trying to believe that she was the one who was finally going to make it all happen for me. And I remember the night I came home from Melon's after meeting Andee. And called you out in California. And Lynn.

I turn and go for my jacket again. I've got to get out of this place. But I look down for no good reason and see some papers in the wastebasket. I pick them up, check them out. Futterman has tried four different notes before he found the tactful way to let me down. Here they are, first draft Dear JJ's, commingling with a rotting apple core and two rubber bands in the trash. Now I'm juiced. How do I know that what he wrote me, what I'm going crazy about, is even the truth? Here are four other versions of the story. I stomp into the master B, tuned for full-scale violation, and immediately lock onto the Man's Fendi valise. I open it and flip through a wad of papers, a package of Kleenex, some file folders, and, to my horror, a hard-boiled egg, and I find what I'm looking for.

"Notes: February 11, re: *The Woman Asleep on the Library Bench*," it says in neat little letters at the top, and other than some reference at the very end to China that I don't understand, it proceeds to trash my play for every reason that I was assured before I even began would not be offered or even debated with regard to this show. They knew what I wanted to do with this story, Deek. And they knew that the form I chose to tell it was more important to me than anything anybody in the play would say. And yet here it is in black and white in front of me: "beginning, middle, and end" bullshit, complaints about the lack of "surprise plot twists" or a "heart-wrenching emotional climax and dénouement." "The play is too episodic," "it's filmlike" (because I'm from LA?) and "can we show rape in the theater, even as part of a true story?" "A Broadway audience must either laugh or cry; thinking alone will not make for a run." "Why does the woman end up on a park bench when she has credit cards?" "The playwright talks of his structure being inspired by Brecht, but who ever made a dime off of Brecht?" "The big arenas have their own rules, honey." And my favorite: "this is still only an outline for a play, at best."

You know something, Deek? Futterman said that to me when we had our very first conversation about the play, before he even optioned it. I let it go by because I wanted to make the deal and I figured I could change his thinking with my enthusiasm for a new form. You'd think I would know by now that the theater is like a marriage and you don't go into it thinking you'll be able to change

171

someone, right? Wrong. And here I am, once again with nothing but my hands in my pockets to prove it.

So I'm burned and abandoned, loved and let loose, drained and pumped, all at the same time. I Xerox Futterman's notes on his Canon, replace them in the valise, grab my jacket, and split into the night.

First stop, The Dakota, where, for the four hundredth time since I got here in January, I stop and linger over the pavement where John Lennon met his bloody end.

Then down and dirty into the subway, where I catch the A train down to Times Square and get off to strut with the hustlers and drug dealers and pimps. A guy offers me some toot and I blow my nose all over the filthy cement in front of him. A couple of black guys laugh and so do I and for the first time in my life I'm not scared out of my mind in this station. Then I hop the next local going downtown and ride between cars for three or four stops watching the wheels make sparks on the rotting tracks. Twice somebody comes through and almost knocks me to my death and I don't give the slightest damn. I get off at Spring Street and eye the blue and white tiles around the station's name on the wall until the train pulls out and all is quiet. But while I'm heading for the exit I realize my time may have come. There near the stairs are two punks in leather jackets, one with an ugly rooster-tail haircut up top, and they separate while advancing toward me. To my surprise, I hike up my collar, put my hands in my jacket pockets, open my eyes wide, and smile. The one with the haircut asks me if I have the time. For what, I say, clenching my fist in my pocket as though I have a gun. The other guy looks toward my hands, shakes his head to his partner, and they run. Fuckin' A, I think, this is the trick, this is what I'm gonna show Futterman next time he sees me. Sweet little California boy, huh? In your face, motherfucker!

I hit the street. I walk over toward Maggie Steinfeld's place thinking maybe I'm going to kill her. I ring her bell

172

when I get there but she's gone. I round a corner, pass some restaurants, stop in front of one called The Charcuterie, and who do I see inside but Matt Stanese with the Angel Andee. They're in a booth toward the back and she's crying. I start to cry. I think of going in, grabbing her, and running for the rest of my life. But I decide we'll never make it through the door. And besides, what am I going to say—that the party's over, Futterman has pulled the plug on our dreams, but let's split anyway? No, better to sweat this night out on my own, let her do what she has to do, which, from appearances, Stanese isn't liking anyway. I turn away and head back up the street.

And on the sidewalk, mixed with the filth and shine of the city ice, the babies and bums, the numbers parlors and hundred-dollar-a-plate restaurants, is my life. One step at a time, worn boots that have trekked through a dozen American cities' streets in search of "the theater" leaving fresh marks in dirty Manhattan snow. All paths have always led to this Roman megalopolis for me. Within shouting distance alone are three theaters that have long professed to want my plays in their wings. Here I am, motherfuckers, I scream. But buildings rich with the echoes of history are totally indifferent to me. I've known the feeling of walking these blocks as though I owned them. The first time was when I visited the city when I was but a dope of twelve. The world seemed to owe me a debt of gratitude back then. Now I seem unable to collect even on some interest.

I stop and look at a painting in the window of a gallery called Toll. On the canvas are three distinct squares of colored stripes. Each square is the same size and of the same composition. And yet each is different. I stare for a while trying to figure out why. Finally I realize that as the stripes move from square to square across the canvas they lose all sense of borders until in the third square they seem to have become just pure color instead of "stripes."

This is what I am trying to do in my play, I think to myself. Strip characters of their ideas of life in tiny squared-off scenes until all that is left by the end is life itself, free of borders, free of expectations, free, perhaps, to renew itself. I wonder if Maggie Steinfeld has ever stopped to look in this window which is two doors down from her apartment. You want to see how someone can end up on a park bench even though they have credit cards in their pocket, Cunt? Come on down here and look at this. I smile at the reflection of my own eyes in the painting and think of a Peter Handke line that has gotten me through more than one night like this: "*I always thought of art as a parachute that would save me from falling.*"

And at this, my eyes close and I am in midair. In free-fall. Wind is rushing by. Pulling all sound right out of my ears. And as I fall, I am wondering if I still believe. And if I am ready to pull the rip cord and find out. Will the parachute still be there? Will it still save me? And if not, what will the final descent be like? Will I be conscious all the way down, even at impact, when I at last explode, like a lifelong dream, in a splatter that once and for all reveals the true shape of my life for all to see? I shut my eyes even tighter. And suck in my breath. To pull or not to pull. *Damn it all—in spite of everything—I still believe!* I pull . . .

Sometime later I find myself riding the AA local again and I have no recollection of how long I've been aboard. I look at my watch and it says 2:15. There's no one in the car but me and a shooter and he's out cold on his face or dead. One shitty light flickers on and off dimly at my end of the car. Two leather fags get on at West 4th, eye the shooter, and think he's a corpse. Then they turn to me and stare. "California," I say to them, before the doors close, and they run back out on the platform in fear. As the train pulls out of the station I start to laugh. The light's flickering, a door is flapping open, the sound is deafening, it's 2:15 in the morning, I'm pretty sure I've lost everything, and I'm thinking, "Safe at last."

Now here I am back in the pull-out at Futterman's. Somebody's out there in the dining room. Must be him or his wife. Or one of the twins. Or the maid. She's from Jamaica and sometimes she gives me my mail when she thinks she might catch a glimpse of something interesting in here. She's afraid of the statues of Futterman and his wife though. She once told me I should cover them while I wrote. Maybe I'll go out there and read her the play out loud. Or what you say in your letter about the triangle of love. Still think yours is the same shape as mine, buddy? I'd be hard pressed to believe it. As for whether I can see myself in the world without Lynn, your question unfortunately is voiced to me a day late. Right now I can't see myself in the world at all.

I said I was sorry they were changing your movie so much, Deek. But maybe they have a point. Maybe the guy should know that he's better off leaving his dreams be dreams. In dreams there are no borders at all.

JJ

Mr. J. J. Towne
c/o Futterman
183 Central Park West
New York, NY 10023

Dear JJ,

It's done. I've been going at it for the last 24 hours with
Matt since I left you sleeping at the hotel. Called in sick
today at work and everything. We made a real scene last
night in a restaurant down here and then took the screaming home with us.

Basically he understands. I'm not saying he likes the
situation—he was really hot about it at first—but he's
accepted the fact that he can't hold on to me against my
will. People change. That's all it amounts to. We were
good for each other for a long time, but all things must
pass, right?

Anyway, he agreed to go away for a while so I can
get my things together and decide what I want to do.
Neither of us wants to keep the loft, so we're going to sell
it. I thought about staying here with you, but the idea
somehow doesn't seem right. I'd rather we decide on
something together, when the time is right. Meanwhile, I
think we're free to see each other. Matt's going to California, at least for now.

Where are you anyway, my love? I've been calling
you for the last hour and a half and I get no answer.
Another few minutes and it'll be Valentine's Day and I
wanted to hear your sweet voice tell me you were mine. I
do love you, JJ. I feel really good about this. I'm going to

go to sleep now and dream about us. Have to be in the studio early tomorrow to cover my shots from today. I'll messenger this·over and try to call you during a break. Maybe we can have dinner. Hope Futterman loved the play.

HAPPY VALENTINE'S DAY, my delicious!

L&K,
Andee

Tuesday, February 14

Mr. Richard Case
27 Saltair Road
Malibu, CA 90233

Dear Deek,

Today being Valentine's Day, I want to let you know what's in my heart. I woke up this morning afraid. I don't know exactly why, but I think it has something to do with us. I take that back—I know it has something to do with us. And JJ. And what's going on with all three.

I haven't heard from him in a long time, you know. I've written and tried to call once or twice, but nothing's come back. That Sunday out at your house, when he called on your machine, was the last time I heard the sound of his voice. Part of me, as you know, hasn't cared. I needed a break from him. I don't have to tell you. Something's been missing. Something that counts. Something I've been finding in you. It's there in the way you look at me. And search me. And probe for what's underneath. For so long now, JJ and I have been content to coast along on the surface. We've become life preservers for each other, really good only for keeping our bobbing apple heads out of the water as the waves of trauma pass. Maybe that's inevitable in a marriage. Maybe not. I hope the day never comes when I believe that's the way it has to be.

But this morning I guess I came close. I just woke up and realized how truly different I've been feeling since I started sleeping with you. My music has come back to me, Deek. And so has my body, my sex. I go through the

178

day feeling more a part of the world, more valuable, more alive. My mind is working again. I'm thinking things and am finding a way to give my thoughts voice. I'm even angry at a lot of what I see around me, which for me is a rejuvenating sensation. I used to be angry at everything and I think I was a better person for it. Sourness isn't what I'm talking about; just a lack of so damn much complacency. I never thought there was a chance I could become an old married cynic, but maybe I was farther down that road than I've cared to admit. Maybe LA has been working on me, too, despite my claims to the contrary over the years. Anyway, whatever the reasons, it's obvious that somewhere along the way I at least stopped asking the right questions.

But I've somehow snapped out of it. That's what I'm saying. And I have you to thank for it. Which is why I feel I have to tell you that this seems like a good place to bring things between us to a stop. I don't want to particularly. And I can't say I'm going to find it very easy. But I think I have to know if it's marriage or me, if I'm feeling so good because I'm free of the person or free of the bond. If it's that JJ and I are lost to each other, as I've suspected while he's been gone on this trip, then maybe you and I can find out if we want each other for real. But if not, if it's that I have to remain free of marriage to feel this way, then I'd better find that out before I get into anything else. Either way, I don't think we should go any further just now. The last thing I'd want would be to mess up what we've had.

In that letter you wrote me last month, when we both woke up feeling all guilty and ashamed that one day, you said you wanted to look at what happened between us as a gift and not let it become less than what it really was. I guess that's all I'm saying now. In your words, I want to savor it, caress it as in a dream, and awake all the better for it in the morning.

So thank you, Deek. You've done nothing less than revive my heart. I hear it beating right now. In the time signature of joy. Who knows? Maybe it's a song to our future. It's definitely no longer a lament for the past.

Happy Valentine's Day, with my love.
Lynn

Tuesday, February 14, Valentine's Day

Crazy today. Woke up afraid, Rudi next to me in the bed staring wide-eyed. Was I talking in my sleep? Dreaming? I remember nothing. Just tossing and turning for the better part of the night, falling asleep only as the sun came up.

Then on the way in to the office, another anxiety attack. Coming over the hill on Coldwater, just before Mulholland, at that stupid rise in the pavement, I suddenly didn't think the road was going to be there on the other side. My heart jumped up in my throat, pounding, my eyes started watering, and I couldn't breathe. I pulled over and thought I was going to throw up. Mouth dry, the shakes, my clothes soaking with sweat, everyone honking. I thought I was going to fucking die again. Of course I didn't know where I was. Just like always, I flashed on some dumb little thing in the past. This time when JJ and I were buying our first car together, the white Fiat back in Ann Arbor. I could hear the salesman's voice and everything. "Will you be paying with cash or time?" "Cash or time." "Cash or time." It kept pounding in my head like a Gregorian chant until I finally came to or at least consciously acknowledged it. Somebody should really look into these things. In my opinion, the secret of time travel may lie in the blood chemistry of a human anxiety attack. You're not remembering something while it's occurring. You are fucking transported.

Anyway, made it in to the office, where David said I looked like death warmed over. I thanked him and slowly returned to sanity as we decided how to do nothing for the remainder of the week.

Then a good-bye Valentine to Deek. I'm not sure where it came from. I hadn't planned it. But it jumped right out of me and did feel honest. I think we are most true to ourselves in two of life's little rites of passage: when we say hello to someone or something and then again when we say good-bye. We like to look forward to life's experiences and then, once we have them under our belt, look back on them with regret. The problem is, my regret over this is borderline panic. I don't think this attack was any coincidence. The ascent of that hill today was the time I've been spending with Deek. Joyous, liberating, forward-looking time. The road that I suddenly thought might just not be there on the other side was JJ. Without much more than a blink of the eye, he could be gone. I could be with someone else. And enjoying it. If that's not frightening, then I don't know what is.

So, even though it hurts, I think I've done the right thing. I feel as if I've awakened from a long sleep, or that Deek has awakened me like a magic prince, and there's no turning back. I want to keep this feeling of being alive in my life even if it means a return of some of the old fears. But I also want to find out if I can keep it with JJ around. I feel I owe it not only to him, but to myself, in spite of all my doubts, to try. We had it once; maybe we can again. If not, Deek has given me the confidence that I can have it with someone else. Maybe even him.

Now . . . how do I get JJ back here to try? Today's project, Ms. Rodnick-Towne: seduce your husband across three thousand miles, four time zones, the NY-LA cultural barrier, the recent sour history of your marriage, and the fact that he has no reason at present to come home to you.

Tuesday afternoon, February 14

Mr. J. J. Towne
c/o Futterman
183 Central Park West
New York, NY 10023

Dear JJ,

Enclosed please find a cassette I recorded the other night—my first piano improv in two and a half years. Something's come back in me and it longs for itself, for what it once was, and what it still could be. It's come out in music and, I think, in a few other ways. Will you listen and tell me if you like what you hear? That would make me very happy.

Happy Valentine's Day, my love. I'm thinking of you.

Always,
Lynn

WESTERN UNION
Los Angeles 555 6B14A 7617606 136 23 150 5460 18333
9.15P 2.14 Tuesday.

MR. J. J. TOWNE
C/O FUTTERMAN
183 CENTRAL PARK WEST
NEW YORK, NY 10023

JJ. LYNN HAS BEEN IN ACCIDENT. HAVE TRIED TO PHONE.
WILL CONTINUE. COME IMMEDIATELY. CEDARS SINAI.
ROOM 809. NOTE FOR YOU AT HOME. DEEK.

8 AM, Wednesday, February 15

Dear Peter,

I'm sorry to leave without saying good-bye, but I have an emergency at home. Lynn was in an accident last night—that's what was in the telegram that came—and I have to be with her.

I appreciate the things you told me about the play Monday night. As you know, I disagree with the basis for much of the criticism, but, as promised, I will attempt to sort it all out as best I can and, now, when I can.

Thank you again for this time in New York and for welcoming me into your home. I am grateful even if the results were not what either of us hoped for. My best to Susie.

Again, I'm sorry for this haste in my departure. I will be in touch.

Sincerely,
JJ

185

Miss Andee O'Neill
121 Chambers St.
New York, NY 10013

Dear Andee,

Impossible as it may seem, I am on a plane home. Just
a few short hours ago I held you as the sun came up,
and now it burns over a long bright wing to my left, at
30,000 feet.

    When I got back to Futterman's, there was a tele-
gram waiting for me. I was stupid enough to think it
was another valentine from you or something, but when
I opened it, my heart sank. Lynn was in an accident
yesterday evening and she's in the hospital with injuries.
I tried to call you but the switchboard said you were
taping and I decided not to leave this in a message. I have
to be with her, Andee. I got the first flight out.

    This is so disorienting. First the disappointment of the
play. Then the wonder of you helping me to regain myself in one short night. I walked back to Futterman's on
air this morning, my jacket wide open, not even feeling the cold. Then this. I don't know what to feel at this
point. All I know is that your being able to say all those
things to me in spite of what happened to my dream of
taking New York by storm is what is propelling me forward. If I didn't have that, this plane would thunder ahead
without me, leaving me to fall to earth in a clump, never
to be heard from again.

    I thank God for you right now and I'm not sure I even

believe in God. Maybe your existence is proof of his. Please wait to hear from me. I'll call just as soon as I possibly can.

I love you. And I thank you. You're mine and I'm yours. I promise I won't forget.

Always,
JJ

Wednesday, February 15, 6 AM

JJ—

I'm leaving this hoping you'll come here first from the
airport. First off, *Lynn's okay*. She's had a rough night but
she's okay. There's a slight concussion and some bruised
ribs, but nothing major. The doctors say she'll need some
rest, but that's about it.

Strange thing is, the police seem to think she was run
off the road up near Coldwater and Mulholland. A
woman in the car behind her got a license number and
swears it looked intentional. Cops were asking all kinds
of questions at the hospital and supposedly they're checking out the car and the report right now. I guess Lynn
kept mumbling my name on the way there in the ambu-
lance, so I got the once-over first. They were very heavy
about where you were and why too. I said nothing about
A, of course. Finally, they let me send the telegram to
you when I assured them you couldn't possibly have had
anything to do with the accident. They were going to
have you questioned in New York, JJ, so don't be surprised if they jump on you a little when you arrive. My
advice is to be a little belligerent. Then they back off.

I'll be there until you arrive. Room 809 West. I'm
sure we'll have some talking to do.

Sorry about this, pal.

Deek

My Lynnie,

I'm sitting here next to you, my love. I've had your hand in mine since I got here. The doctors asked me not to wake you, at least for today. They say it's natural for your body to want rest and that you may sleep for a couple of days. But you're fine, that's the important thing. They're sure of that.

I'm leaving you this note because I have to talk with the police about what happened and do a few other things. They seem to think somebody caused the accident and they have some information for me. I got the first plane out of New York and, needless to say, I'm glad to be here. Deek's been here too. I guess, right from the start. You were smart to ask for him. The nurses all tell me he's been great. I finally got him to go home at least for a nap.

Anyway, I'll be back just as soon as I can. If you do wake up, please ask the nurse to get in touch with me immediately. She'll know where.

To look at you, you'd never know anything was wrong. You look so pretty and sweet. It's hard to believe it's only six weeks since I saw you last. It seems like a year. Or a lifetime. New York does that to you, I guess. But I'm here now. Don't worry, everything will be all right. Somehow.

JJ

THE BEVERLY HILLS HOTEL

Wed, February 15

Mr. J. J. Towne
8541 Coldwater Canyon
Los Angeles, CA 90056

Towne—

Read in the paper your wife had an accident. Sorry to hear that, although I'm sure you two were glad to see each other, even under the circumstances. Just think, it could have been worse, right?

I'm at the Beverly Hills Hotel. Not far from where you live, I understand. Maybe you'd want to stop by for some lunch. I have a few things I'd like to discuss with you.

Look forward to seeing you. My best to your wife.

Matt Stanese

Deek—

I need to talk to you. I'm down the road at Moonshadows. Lynn's fine, still sleeping like a baby, but believe it or not, I got a note from Stanese. He's at the Beverly Hills Hotel and he wants to see me. Says he read about the accident in the paper, but between the lines I think he's saying something else. Shit, Deek, I don't know whether to go or to call the police or what. I'll wait for you at the restaurant. Please come as soon as you get back.

JJ

PETER FUTTERMAN

Thursday, 2/16

Mr. J. J. Towne
8541 Coldwater Canyon
Los Angeles, CA 90056

Dear JJ,

I've tried numerous times to reach you by phone, but having no success, I decided finally to write. I was shocked and sorry to hear about Lynn and I pray that she is all right. As you know, I so liked her from our brief meeting out there at the hotel. Please give her my best wishes for a speedy recovery and know that my prayers are with you both.

I'm sorry to see your time in New York end in this way. You were not alone in hoping for more. But keep your faith, JJ. You're a very talented writer and talent will out. If good things come to those who wait, I will await further word from you.

My sincere best wishes to you.

Peter

P.S. I am returning the enclosed package which arrived for you here by UPS today.

Thursday, February 16

J. J. Towne
8541 Coldwater Canyon
Los Angeles, CA 90056

Dear JJ,

I wanted to write before I lost the sound of your voice, which is still in my ear. All that noise on the phone made you seem so far away. But then, you are, aren't you? I can't believe all this has happened when I still have the feel of you inside me from just two nights ago.

JJ, I'm sorry about Matt. I don't know whether he is responsible for Lynn, but please don't push him to find out. I'd rather you let him think we were never going to see each other again than make him feel he has to prove something more. That note was a threat. Believe me, I know how he operates. The best thing you could do right now is just let him know that you got it. Please trust me. Going to the police would accomplish nothing. It might even make matters worse. Whatever he has in mind, I'm sure I'll hear from him before too long and I'll handle him somehow. Okay? I've got to know that you're going to listen to me. That's why I took the chance of writing this even though we agreed I wouldn't send letters to your house.

I guess it's going to be harder than we thought, huh . . . ? It's certainly now going to take time. But I can wait. You're worth it to me. Just promise you won't let the distance that now separates us find its way into your heart. I heard it in your voice a little tonight and it scared me.

Then again, I can imagine what you must be going through there. You have it all to deal with for real. Just know that I'm here if you need me. Waiting. And wanting. Matt's dealt the cards that are going to break him. He just doesn't know it yet because they're in our hands. And we're going to play them together.

Call me when you can. I wish I could be there to help you. I *am* glad Lynn's okay.

I love you so.
Andee

Friday

Mr. Richard Case
27 Saltair Road
Malibu, CA 90233

Deek—

Talked to Andee last night and she agreed with you re:
how to handle our fucked friend from the east. Enclosed is
a copy of the thing he sent me as well as what I'm sending
over to the hotel this morning, just in case there are any
more "accidents" before I see you next.
  I'll be at the hospital all day.

JJ

195

Friday, February 17

Mr. Matt Stanese
c/o The Beverly Hills Hotel
9641 W. Sunset Blvd.
Beverly Hills, CA 90210

Dear Stanese,

I got your note and I'm touched by your concern for my wife. Of course you'll understand if I decline the luncheon invitation while I remain at her side in the hospital. Perhaps another time.

You're correct in saying that our reunion was joyful, even under the circumstances. Home is where the heart is, as they say. Hope you find your way back to yours with no further delay.

Best wishes.

JJ Towne

They tell me it's Friday. And that I'm in Cedars Sinai. Which, along with the rest, explains why I feel hopelessly lost.

For two days I've been hallucinating that I was a runner whose feet were leaving tracks of musical notes across staff paper that was forming a document linking all forms of twentieth-century music with the Brandenburg Concertos. Bach himself was watching me with amusement as I conjured up living, singing proof. For instance, John Lennon would float by singing that nonsense love song off *Abbey Road,* "Quando para mucho mi amore te felice corazon, Mundo paparazzi mi amore chica fair le parasol, Questo abrigado tanta mucho cake and the tin carousel" and I would trace the notes of Lennon's singing by running them across the paper and this would make Bach laugh. Segue into Stravinsky's "Rite of Spring" mixed with Mick Jagger skipping along cooing, "Oo, oo, oo, oo, oo, oo, oo; Oo, oo, oo, oo, oo, oo, oo, Lord I miss you" to be followed by Greg Kihn crying, "My love's in jeopardy, My love's in jeopardy, oooo, oo, oo, oo." (Bach liked this one.) Then the hiss of Berlin doing "Sex" would start up, but Chrissie Hynde would take over, lamenting, "I went back to Ohio, but my city was gone," and at this The Clash would jump in for what seemed like days with "Hey, you got to let me know, Should I stay or should I go?" followed loudly by Translator pleading, "I thought I felt your touch, in my car on my clutch, But I guess it was just someone, who felt a lot like I remember you do, 'Cause you're in New York and I'm not, Yeah, you're everywhere that I'm not, I'm not, I'm not" and finally mellowing into a joyous round which mixed an ever-spiraling Yeatsian double vortex on synthesizer by Philip Glass with Musical Youth laughing their way through

"Pass the Dutchie." So imagine my surprise, upon finally opening my eyes, when before me, in a hospital room, in a hospital chair, next to a hospital bed, which I (also to my surprise) lay in, sat my husband asking me if I was all right.

The sight of JJ's face is always something to be reckoned with. He used to be so young-looking that people would mistake us for brother and sister (me being the older of the two, of course), but he's changed in the last couple of years, started getting gray around the temples, and since he's been playing voracious amounts of tennis he's bulked up about the shoulders and thighs. When we were married, they carded us for drinks in New York City (where the drinking age was 18) and stuffed us into innocuous corners of restaurants. Now when we walk into a place, we get the best table and I'm lucky if we get out without a cocktail waitress slipping him her phone number. He's at once elegant and boyish-looking, refined and mischievous. His hair is thick and his hips are thin. His voice is soft like a child's, but his eyes can cut right through you like razors. He can disarm you, comfort you, and scare you all at the same time. In short, he can be very attractive.

When I first saw him sitting there, I thought nothing of it. I'm in a hospital, I said to myself, and my husband is at my side. But then I looked around, wondered what hospital, and why. And whether I was hallucinating JJ as I had hallucinated Bach. Or if not, where he had come from. And I tried to move. Which brought it all home. In the clear language of pain.

When I left the office Tuesday afternoon I remember thinking that maybe I should drive back home a different way, avoid the scene of that morning's demons up in the canyon near Mulholland. But I resisted, remembering a doctor's advice given me long ago when the anxiety attacks used to hit me with disturbing regularity. "It's like

198

falling off a horse," he said, "the sooner you get back up and ride through the trouble spot, the sooner you'll put it behind you." This advice was obviously spoken by a man who had never experienced one of these attacks. When given the choice, there isn't a human being alive who wouldn't pick a horse, even a bucking bronco, over the invisible dread of death from within, which is the way one of these things makes you feel.

But I pressed on anyway, aimed my car at ground zero like a soldier valiantly going off to war. And I thought I was doing fine. In fact, I thought I was home free, when this fucking red Pinto (ah, irony . . .) comes flying out of nowhere from the Mulholland side of the fork at the top of the hill and gives me the choice of oncoming traffic or the Tree People sign. (Who are the Tree People anyway?) Naturally I chose the sign. Which landed me here in the hospital for what I now know was my morphine-induced sojourn into one woman's musicology. Listen, if that's a concussion experience, I'm here to testify that it's better than a whole lot of drugs I've done in my time.

Anyway, I'm face-to-face with a beautiful JJ and he's leaning over me telling me I'm fine and giving me this note that says everything is going to be fine, which is fine with me, except that there's an echo in my head and it feels like someone's sitting on my chest about to crush me. I try to speak but JJ puts a finger to my lips. "Rest," he whispers, and then he kisses me softly.

I close my eyes again and remember the first time JJ kissed me. After that night at the bookstore with the Mark Strand poem, when I took him home with me to my apartment back in Ann Arbor, we were laying on the green carpet floor looking at these crayon drawings I had done in the first grade. They were funny drawings and though I had them with me always, I rarely showed them to anyone. But for JJ, I had taken out the red and white cigar box that I kept them in and he was laughing his sweet little boy laugh while telling me what he thought the drawings meant. One showed a tiny frightened girl running down a hill to her father's outstretched arms at the bottom. "I need food and shelter," the caption read. Another showed the girl crying next to her mother, who had her back turned and was looking at the sky. "Also warmth and love," the little crayon markings cried out. JJ had filled in all the blanks, detailing somehow exactly what it was like to grow up in the bizarre household of my childhood, where my mother would have nothing to do with me and my father crossed gender constantly to do all providing. I smiled, not believing he could draw so much insight from a few simple drawings. And then he looked deep into my eyes and kissed me. "I can give you what you need," he said, "and more." And the next thing I knew we were in my bed, under the navy comforter, and he was inside me forever.

Now in a hospital bed twelve years later, the same kiss was just a reason for memories. I guess that was yesterday, because the sun seems to have come and gone and come again. Along with JJ. And today we talked.

"What are you doing here, playwright?" I said, grinning, when he strolled in.

"I was going to ask you the same question."

"This is where they put people who run their cars into signposts."

"Yeah, and this is where they put their husbands." JJ smiled as he dropped into the green armless chair next to my bed. "The police say it wasn't your fault, you know."

"That's a switch."

"Yeah." JJ laughed. "Might be good for insurance, too, but . . ."

At this, he trailed off. And I got my first whiff of what was to come. I don't think you're ever really ready to hear stuff like this, even if you've suspected it and prepared yourself for it, and even if you're no stranger to it yourself.

But I guess JJ was full with it and couldn't wait to get it off his chest. He dumped it all right out there on the bed and we just sat and looked at it and at each other for what felt like the rest of the day.

Seems while I was out at the beach cavorting with his best friend, he was falling head over heels for a 22-year-old model soap star Mafiosa princess. The long silences between calls and letters were due not only to his time at the rewrite desk but to misplaced nights and stolen afternoons with his Juliet of the Soapsuds. I listened and listened. And then listened some more. She was dark and very pretty, inexperienced and young, filled with enthusiasm and a thirst for living—all very much the opposite of me (according to JJ). And for JJ, she was a chance at a renewed life. She wanted him and he wanted her. It was already decided. I knew JJ was suffering to have to do this to me on my sickbed, but I guess he felt the sooner he got it over with, the better.

By the time he finished, I felt almost sorry for him. I mean, here he was sitting here looking better than he has in his entire life. He'd had an incredible winter in Fat City, living it up, thinking he was about to enter the realm of possibilities he had dreamt of for years, possibilities which I had prayed for *with* him, and within a period of 72 hours the whole thing had come down like a house of cards in a sudden wind. The play was dead. Everyone hated the work he had done (although to me it sounds terrific). He had been betrayed by a duplicitous director. (He doesn't even know about his producer . . .) His lust for Abie's Irish Rose had placed his life in jeopardy (and mine, too, as I was later to find out). And he'd had to run out on everyone at the summons of a telegram from his best friend that placed his wife in a hospital with unspecified injuries from an unexplained accident.

Unexplained, that is, until he arrived back at home and heard talk of my car being forced off the road. And then received a little explanatory word from the keeper of the princess, Mr. Mafioso himself, who was apparently at the Beverly Hills Hotel even as we spoke.

"So I want you to tell the police you have no memory of any car pushing you off the road," JJ said in earnest. "It won't do us any good to push this any further. Even Deek agrees."

"Deek?" I asked faintly. "What does he know about this?"

"Everything," JJ answered. "I've been writing him."

"The whole time?"

"He's my friend, Lynnie. I had to tell someone."

And so, there it was. Not only had I been betrayed by my husband, but also by his best friend, whom I had been betraying my husband with. I'm sitting here thinking during this whole sob story that I'm not even going to say anything, that I'm just going to go straight to the beach when I get out of this formaldehyde dump and fuck my brains out in the surf for about a year and a half, or until I get over JJ, whichever comes first, and let him think what he will when he finds out. But lo and behold, I'm the one who finds out. Deek has known from the beginning of JJ's dalliance with the princess of the daytime airwaves. Probably got his rocks off on the whole idea, too, while watching the little bitch on his tube. Maybe even while he was fucking me. Or watching me squirm in the dank claws of guilt. And all while talking to me of love. And a goddamn novel of roses and reconciliation.

Well, fuck me! It seems to be the national pastime at the moment. My husband, Deek, even some goon from Little Italy that I've never laid eyes on who's playing with my life over his obsession with Suzy Soapslut, who he picked out of the gutters of Boston and made into a star.

"Fuck me! Do you hear me?! Fuck me good!" I screamed.

And a bunch of the folks in white did hear. They

came running in from the hallway with their pills and needles and arm restraints and everything. And while JJ watched and, if memory serves, even shed a tear or two, they shot me up and right back to Brandenburg and Mr. J. S. Bach himself, who turned to me smiling after a long organ intro and welcomed me back by singing in sweet dulcet tones, "My love's in jeopardy, jeopardy, jeopardy, baby, oooo, oo, oo, ooooooooooooooooo . . ." At which point the lights went right out.

Saturday, February 18

Lynn Towne
Room 809 West
Cedars Sinai Hospital
8700 Beverly Blvd.
Los Angeles, CA 90048

Dear Lynn,

I can only guess at the reasons why you had me removed from your visitors list. Please let me try to explain.

I know you know about JJ now. I guess you also know that he's been talking to me about New York all along. Which must make you think I took advantage of the situation to take advantage of you.

If that's it, Lynn, I have to tell you you're wrong. I did know what JJ was doing back there. He wrote me about the girl and I wrote him back. But our letters were letters about friendship. Mostly, ours. We got into love and marriage some, true, but it was really by way of comparing the different choices each of us has made down the line.

When you came over that first afternoon, I didn't plan on anything happening. Think about it. I said to come out, sure, but if my memory is right, it was you who called me saying you felt like some company. I was happy to oblige. But could I have made Rudi roll in seaweed covered with tar so that she would need that bath? Could I have planned on the sunset? Or on you pouring that beer all over me? And looking at me the way you did? About the only thing I could have planned on, I suppose, was you looking as good as you did. But even there I would have been wrong. As long as I live, I'll never forget the sight of you in that bathtub, all sunburnt, your golden hair falling damp across your redbrown back, your suit falling to the tiles, the foam on the beer covering and then falling from your breasts, and us falling to the water, to my bed, to the night, to where we are right now. You never looked like that before, Lynn. Not to me.

And I didn't use you. Or the situation. If I had wanted to do that, I think I *would* have told you about JJ. To be honest, I didn't know what his affair was going to lead to. I don't have to tell you that things haven't been right with him. You've both been saying it for a long time. And I agreed. And I've told JJ as much. But I thought maybe he was just groping for a way to find out what he wanted. He's gone looking before. You know that. And usually what it does is make him appreciate you all the more.

But I confess, I was starting to think this thing with Andee might be different. He was saying it was making him feel like he could renew himself, recover his sense of purpose, and that he liked thinking that. So I encouraged him. I honestly thought I owed it to him as a friend to do that. But nowhere in my mind was a lack of concern for you. Even if JJ ran off with Andee the happiest man on earth, I thought it was better than leaving things between you two as they were before he left. I think even you'd agree with that. You've been telling me as much every time you came out to my house.

Lynn, you said the other day that what you needed to know was whether your troubles were in you or in your marriage. You said you were feeling more alive during this time with me than you've felt in years. Why should that be any different now that you know JJ was trying to answer the same question for himself? Do you really think that what happened between us wasn't real? That it wasn't just what we thought it was, felt it was, said it was?

You and I slept together before JJ slept with Andee in

New York, you know. I can prove that to you. About the only thing I can't prove, unfortunately, is what has truly been in my heart for the past seven weeks. When I got your valentine the other day, I think I really found out. The tears it brought to my eyes were real. The way I've admitted to myself that I want you is real. The way I'm feeling shut out right now is very real too.

Lynn, I don't know how this mess is going to work out in the end, but I do know that I have more than just a friend's interest at this point. What you and I have shared with each other these past two months goes beyond mere friendship. It can never be that simple between us again.

Please call me, or see me, or at least write me. I can't do what now has to be done—for you or for me—by myself. And neither can you.

Love,
Deek

Saturday, February 18

Lynn Towne
Room 809 West

Lynnie,

I'm downstairs and I've just been told that, at your request, I'm not to be allowed up to see you as of today. No doubt, it's because of what's happened. Or the fact that I told you about what's happened. I don't blame you, I guess. It's just, I wish you'd let me see you through the hospital stuff at least. I feel so damn responsible for your being here in the first place that it's going to hurt doubly if you don't let me do anything to help you. I promise I won't dump any more surprises on you. Maybe I was wrong to hit you with all that so fast in the first place. I should have let you come through this and at least get back on your feet. I'm sorry, Lynnie. I really am. I feel like a jerk. I didn't sleep at all last night. I kept seeing your sweet eyes looking up at me from that damn hospital bed. I don't know, I'm really confused right now. Please just let me up there. We have to see each other. We have a lot to work out and talk about. And after all these years, we owe it to each other to do it face-to-face. You'll probably find this hard to believe, but I honestly never meant to hurt you.

I still love you.

JJ

Saturday, February 18

Mr. J. J. Towne
8541 Coldwater Canyon
Los Angeles, CA 90056

Dear JJ,

I'm touched by your concern and I'm sorry if feeling responsible for putting me in the hospital is causing you such pain. Maybe you'd like a concussion and a couple of cracked ribs instead. I doubt that would hurt quite so much.

As for what we owe each other, I don't think you're in a position to talk about that at the moment. Neither am I, really. This winter is going to be a turning point in both our lives, JJ. So much has happened. And believe me, there's as much that you don't know about as there is light in the sun. I honestly didn't have a clue as to how I was going to fill you in on what I've been going through here by myself. I just sent you a package the other day that was some sort of attempt to scratch the surface (I think . . .). What I expected from it seems at the moment to have slipped my mind though.

But I do know this accident complicates everything. Pain has its own set of rules. It demands one's undivided attention. It takes away choice. In fact, it makes yesterday's choices, which had attained, at least in memory, the status of trial and tribulation, into today's luxuries. I yearn for yesterday's difficulties at the moment, JJ.

So don't preach to me about what we owe each other right now, okay? I don't want you to see me in a hospital bed. And, maybe more important, I don't want to see you. It hurts too much. Because—surprise, surprise—you looked so good to me. The winter agreed with you. In spite of the way you think it's ended. And it agreed with me. In spite of the way you think I'm laid up. So let's avoid the complication of appearances for the time being, huh? Let's be in touch the way we have been. On paper. Let's try to stay the people each of us had decided we wanted to be. Only let's also be honest with each other about those people. Let's see what *they* would say to each other if given the opportunity. Deal? Then maybe we'll see about face-to-face.

Please give Rudi a kiss from me. She must be as confused as we are.

Lynn

P.S. Don't worry, I told the police this morning that I remembered nothing about any second car. I said I just lost control coming over the rise at Mulholland. Hope that makes your greaseball friend happy.

Saturday, February 18

Mr. Richard Case
27 Saltair Road
Malibu, CA 90233

Dear Deek,

I got your letter and I'm really torn as to how to answer.
On the one hand, I accept what you say and can't deny
that what happened between us meant a lot to me. On
the other hand, you fucking lied to me, Deek. If not
straight out, then by omission. You say it hurts to feel shut
out. Well, I'm sorry, but somehow that seems appropriate
to me. Not telling someone the whole truth shuts them
out too. From reality. You seem to think that's okay if it's
done in the name of keeping experience pure, so pretend
that's what I'm doing. I want you to experience the pain
I'm in with purity. I was flying and now I'm confined to a
starched bed with two cracked ribs and a spinning head,
to say nothing of the damage to my heart.

I believe you didn't want to hurt me. I don't really
want to hurt you either. It's just that out in the big, bad
world of the living you can't keep experience under glass,
like a chapter safely tucked away inside one of your
novels. Even in a novel, for that matter, you can't fuck
someone on page 50 without repercussions on page 200.
In trying to keep our involvement pure, Deek, you turned
it into deception. Which is just what happens in marriage.
It's what happened, in fact, to JJ and me.

Yes, I said I wanted to find out if the fault was in
marriage or me. But how much different is that from
asking if it's in the stars or us? Everyone wants to know

210

this, Deek. Including you. If I were a character in one of your books, you might put these very words in my mouth but you'd also probably stop and wonder who was asking questions of whom. Is the creator talking or is his creation? And if both are filled with questions, who has the answers? Turn the page, right? Maybe we'll both find out.

And please understand, if I don't want to see you right now, it isn't necessarily because I think I can solve anything on my own. It's just that I feel the need to *be* alone. I have wounds to heal before I can think about answers to questions. Physical pain shuts you out from your *life*. The only question is whether the hurt will go away and when. When I can answer that, I'll try to answer the rest.

The nurses all tell me you sat with me straight through the night when I was first brought in. I wouldn't want our last night together to be one I have no memory of because one thing I am sure of now is that what you don't know *can* hurt you. But thanks, Deek. Somewhere deep inside I'm glad you were there.

Lynn

Matt Stanese, you are the lowest. How dare you come in here like that in the middle of the night! What did you hope to find? Me in bed with someone? You know JJ is in California. You saw to that, didn't you? Or maybe you thought I'd be lying here wishing you were back, wishing I hadn't let you go. Well, no such luck, you fucking pig. I wouldn't wish that on my worst enemy. And after what you did out there to JJ's wife, I'll never so much as look at you again. Do you understand me? We're finished. It's over. I want nothing to do with you. Nothing. Take your stuff and disappear. If you and all this crap are not out of here by the end of the day, I'm going straight to the police and I'm going to tell them everything. About you and your friends. About the "accident" in California. About everything. Is that clear? I want you the hell out of my life and I want you out now. I don't ever want to see your face again. It's over. We're finished. I'm on my own. You're gone. *Capice?*

Andee

Sunday

My Andee,

Why so angry? I accept that you don't want to live with me for the time being. I said I would let you have the place. I told you, I only came to say hello, pick up a few things. I'm sorry if I frightened you. I won't do it again. Here, I'm leaving my key. See?

Please, honey, don't be like this. There's no point to it. Even if we aren't together for a while, that doesn't mean we can't be friends. I can still do you good. Believe me. As for Towne's wife, I thought I was doing you a favor. The sooner she knew about you, the better, I thought. You have to believe me, I didn't want her hurt. That was not part of anybody's plan. We just wanted to get her attention. So she'd listen to us. A little near-miss. That's what we had in mind. And then a nice talk by the side of the road. She's the one who ran the car into the post. There was no reason for her to do that. Unless she wanted to. Maybe the woman's fucked up. Maybe she wanted to have an accident for some reason. Maybe she knew about you. How do you know? The other person knows when this kind of thing happens in a relationship. I can vouch for that. Maybe I can vouch for what she did too. I felt like that myself, to tell you the truth, when I first found out about you and Towne. The human mind works in mysterious ways.

Anyway, I'm just saying, don't be so tough on me. You've hurt me enough. Don't make me want to hurt you

213

back. You relax. I'm taking my things. I'm moving out of your life. But I'll always be there. And I'll always take you back. When the day comes that you see you've made a mistake, you just pick up the phone and you're back, no questions asked. Understand? I can always forgive. You have to in this life if you expect to see another day.

All my love always,
Matty

Mr. J. J. Towne
8541 Coldwater Canyon
Los Angeles, CA 90056

Dear JJ,

I'm giving you these notes because . . . I don't know—I can't even say it. I know Matt would never do anything to me. At least I'm pretty sure. But then, I never thought he'd do anything like he did to Lynn either. It's a cardinal sin to do something like that that isn't business. As for what he claims about the accident, I'm sure it's shit. Why would she want to run herself off a road? She didn't know about us at the time, right?

Anyway, as you can see, we finally got it over with. But not without another major screamer. You wouldn't believe what he did. He just walks in here in the middle of the night Saturday, while I'm asleep and everything, and he tries to get into bed with me. I thought it was a burglar at first. If I'd had a gun, I probably would have shot him. So we end up screaming until a neighbor comes down and asks if everything is all right. But he just can't get it into his head that I really want him out of my life. Finally, when the sun comes up, I write him this note and walk out while he's sleeping on the couch.

JJ, I'm so sorry that all this had to happen. And I'm scared. You're so far away. I feel I can't even talk to you when just a short week ago I swore I'd never let you out of my sight. I miss your sweet voice in my ear. I ache for it. Please call me whenever you can. Even if it's during the day, at the show. I just have to talk to you. I need you. I want you. I love you.

Yours forever,
Andee

DOT PENNER

Sunday, February 19

Mr. J. J. Towne
8541 Coldwater Canyon
Los Angeles, CA 90056

Dear JJ,

I've been wanting to write all week. Andee's filled me in on all that's going on, and believe me, you've been in my thoughts. I'm really sorry to hear what happened out there with your wife. I hope she's okay.

I'm also sorry that you had to leave on such a sour note with the play, but I find in the theater that one never knows which blessings arrive in disguise. Maggie *has* gone up to Connecticut to do that play I told you about, so I would take her criticism of the work you did with a grain of salt. As you know, I agreed with some of what she said, but there's also no doubt that she had an interest in seeing to it we didn't go forward with a production right now. As for Futterman, I wouldn't be surprised if he had something else cooking too. I've heard things, but you would probably know more about him than I.

Both Andee and Matt have been over here at different times during various episodes of their split, so I at least know you have that to be happy about. Matt's been upset, but the Rabbit has been very good with him and you should know that Rabbit now realizes he was wrong to try and step in between you two. When he saw how much Andee really wanted you, he had to admit he was viewing the situation rather narrowly and from Matt's point of view. He even thinks that before too much longer you won't have to worry about being with her here in town.

So, be in touch. Let me know what's happening and if there's anything I can do for you. Andee sure misses you. I don't think I've ever seen her this way over a guy. And God knows she's had the opportunities. Whatever you did, you did it right, and though I'm sorry that people had to get hurt, I am happy to see her this way. Congratulations. I really hope you two work out.

Best,
Dot

Monday, February 20

Mrs. Lynn Towne
Room 809 West
Cedars Sinai Hospital
8700 Beverly Blvd.
Los Angeles, CA 90048

Dear Lynnie,

I did something last night. Something I have to find a way to tell you about.

I was just sitting here in the house playing with Rudi. Endless flips of a tennis ball from one end of the living room to the other with her trotting back, the ball in her mouth, tail wagging like all was right in the world. She does wonder where you disappeared to, but I think she's assumed that this is the way it is right now, that she's to have us only one at a time. So I started talking to her, trying to explain things, and that's when it started. The sound of my own voice in the room scared me. It was like I hadn't spoken for months and all of a sudden some croak just popped out. I guess it might have been the room, or me being unaccustomed to it, but Rudi looked at me for a second like I was a stranger, and I'm telling you, my heart jumped into my throat.

So I got up to look for a way out. I mean, it's an odd sensation to feel the walls of your own home closing in on you. I thought maybe I'd call Deek, or you, see if you'd talk to me over the telephone. And that's when I saw this little package I had set on the counter and forgotten about. Futterman forwarded it to me from New York. It was the one you sent me the day of the accident. With

219

your tape inside. I opened it, read your Valentine note, and put the tape on my Walkman. And I've been sitting here on the deck out back ever since. Right through the night with the moon and the wind and our owl, who, I'm glad to see, is still around, and on into the world coming back to life with the heat of the sun this morning. And that's what I feel your music did inside of me—brought back a light where there has been a void.

You know, we've talked at times about what it was doing to you to give up your music the way you did and whether the advantages outweighed the damage. If anybody understands why you felt you had to step back from it, it's me. But to have all this inside of you and to do nothing with it—it just isn't right. I must have listened to the second piece on the tape, the one you call "The Circle Song," twenty times. Do you know how amazing it is? It's one of your minor key rounds that feels to me like the emotional pulse of everything we've been through but haven't spoken about in the last year and a half. Your left hand plays two hearts beating relentlessly, at times in sync, at times out, but always aware of each other, while the right hand dances all the circles of hope and joy and disappointment that those hearts have been hit with out in the world. Listening to this piece, you start feeling manic, like you're going to have to get up out of your chair and dance, only to find that your joy is but a false start replaced by a wash of sadness. It's the sensation we both went through when my play died up in Seattle last year, isn't it? I couldn't describe it any better if I sat down and carved a novel of the experience myself.

Then in "Melted," those long silences which you use to modulate keys are *our* silences, aren't they? All the unspoken hurt, the stuff we couldn't talk about or even face yet another time, lives in those silences. They feel to me like our house at 4:00 in the afternoon, when another day of work is drawing to a close and we're wondering which it's going to lead to—unimagined pleasure or yet more unwished for unhappiness.

God, I'm amazed at you for knowing how to say these things. I think if I could find the emotional equivalent of your notes in words and somehow put it on paper, my problems would be over. But it's not that simple, is it? Especially now, after what's happened this winter.

You know, I remember back in Ann Arbor, after I first met you, when I saw you working on a piece and realized for the first time in my life that music could actually be written on paper the way words were, and it seemed so much purer to me, as though the notes were direct sensations of the heart and yet connected to the mind by the writing process. I remember being amazed and feeling enlightened and in the presence of a great gift that was not only yours but was also something I could accept as a present to me. You showed me that the heart and mind could be connected and that music could be the result. And I vowed never to forget that, Lynnie. And to make my writing as pure and as simple as that.

But I did forget. Time kept passing and I kept trying to grab it, stop it, make it wait for me. And my writing has become, I think, this chase of time. All I really wanted was to produce something that felt like my life to me. The way your tape felt like my life as I listened to it last night. Much to my regret, I haven't succeeded. Not the way you have. I guess when you chase time you always think it's around the next corner, and pretty soon you lose sight of the fact that you're running around the block in an endless circle.

Lynnie, I love you. In spite of everything I said to you the other day. In spite of everything that's happened this winter. In spite of what I've done to you. And to myself. I had some fun. There was physical pleasure, the stuff I can't ever seem to say no to. But I know something right this minute that I want to vow never to forget, what I've known since before I even met you, since back when I used to long for you and wonder who and where you even were. It's that you're my only person. The one I was meant to be with. The one who feels what I feel. And can make those feelings into something I can touch. And, in doing so, touch me. It's true art, what you do, Lynnie. And it saves me truly. After it touches me, I can live.

Now, how do I convince you that this is so after what I've done? How do I get you back? How do I even have the nerve to tell you that I want you back, that I could never live without that music of yours in my ears? That you have to write it, play it, live it in order to be who you really are? That I'd do anything to see that you never give it up again? Or that I give up on you again? Or cause you to give up on me? How do I say that, Lynnie? How do I touch your heart like you've touched mine?

I think I'm still your person too. Can I hope against hope that if I say, simply and from *my* heart, just this one thing, that it might make it true again?

Please say it can be so.

Always,
JJ

Tuesday, February 21

Mr. J. J. Towne
8541 Coldwater Canyon
Los Angeles, CA 90056

Goddamn you, JJ! Goddamn you! Goddamn you! Goddamn you! I'm lying here in a hospital bed, shot full of drugs, with pain as sharp as a knife slicing through my chest every time I breathe, with water and Jell-O the only food I can keep down without getting sick all over myself, with a battery of crazed nurses who treat me as though I'm the crazy one, with a husband who flies across the country and marches in here to tell me that he, the great intellect, the savior apparent to the throne of the American theater, has fallen for a girl on the cover of *Soap Opera Digest*, a girl whose psychotic gangster godlover put me here in this bed in the first place, a girl who was ten when we fitted ourselves with wedding bands that we can't even get on our fingers anymore, a girl who's sucked my husband away from me and who's caused his voice to ring in my ears like a taunt, and now you, my husband, tell me you want me back and you ask me to say it can be so? Maybe you're the crazy one. Maybe you belong in this bed shot up with Percodan. Maybe putting an echo on your words would allow you to hear what *you're* saying.

What am I supposed to think, JJ? What am I supposed to believe? What makes you think I even want to believe? What makes you think I don't already believe? What makes you think I could ever believe? I told you there's as much that you don't know as there is light in the sun and you come to me with this tale of your lies and now your

223

truth and then you claim that we still belong together as one. What voice are you speaking in today, JJ? The failed playwright? The failed lover? Or the perennially hopeful playwright? And the misguided but triumphant lover? Or, I'm sorry, was it the lover of music who heard the harmony of the spheres? Or perhaps just the lover of the spheres? The ones below the shoulders—any pair will do—the just plain lover who loves to get out there on the blessed, loving road?

I fucked my way through the winter, too, JJ. Surpriiiise! I fucked and sucked and devoured, beat, and treated myself to someone else's meat. I bet I came twice to every one of your 22-year-old's little gushes. I grabbed onto someone else's cock and rode it into the night. I rode bareback and used spurs. I soared under the stars. I let him do me and then do me and then do me some more. And then I did myself. In front of him. While he watched. And I watched him. You think I was just sitting here, your little god's angel with wings, tinkling the ivories in a plaintiff cry for your ear when in reality I was getting it up my sweet, blond angel rear. And loving it, JJ. Do you hear me? I loved every minute of it. Sex that was again sex. Instead of a love sonnet for the unable to be born. For the sad little boy that couldn't become, through me or himself, the figure he always figured himself to be. When was the last time we even mentioned the word to each other, JJ? S-E-X. There it is. Itsy, bitsy, little word. Time-honored battleground of a three-letter tiny word. We used to do it honor. We used to speak its praise. Let others think we were the angels. When the lights were out, we used to be depraved.

What happened, do you suppose? Two people couldn't be more right for each other than we were. Mind and body, spirit and flesh—we were the perfect fit. Unique. Unlike all who passed before us, and all who would pass after. There were stones in the sea that only we had seen.

Is it just marriage? Are we ready to admit we can't prove everyone wrong and make it work? Have we taken our place in line, become one of "them," against our best intentions, against our own will, against the very beat of our hearts? Or is it us? Have we become someone—or something—other than we know, other than we even want to know?

I've wondered about these things all winter myself, JJ. You weren't alone in feeling the need for rebirth. If it's true that you heard a chronicle of our descent in the music on my tape, then I've at least found my way of giving our broken heart its voice. But that doesn't change the story of that heart. Or its breaking. You're right when you say we haven't talked since Seattle. And that was a year ago. What exactly happened up there anyway? After your incredible three-month silence, you never really explained. I have my ideas but I'd like to hear it from you. Is that asking too much? If so, I don't care. I'm asking anyway. Because I'm so disappointed. And angry. At you. And at myself. We slipped silently into regret during those months and, in my opinion, that's a slide that you don't get off. Instead, you just keep slipping faster and faster down. First comes winters like this, with their accidents and hospitals and brushes with pain. After that, who knows? Maybe the end. Again and again.

Remember what we promised ourselves way back when we first discussed even the idea of getting married, JJ? *No regrets—ever.* We swore it. Sealed it with a kiss. We shook on it before we walked down the aisle. And now look at us. Writing letters back and forth because we can't even bear to look into one another's eyes and speak the truth.

I hate you for this, JJ. And I hate myself. Because goddamn you and goddamn it, I still love you and want you too. In spite of it all. And that's not fair. Or right. Or even what I expected. It's only the truth. The goddamn,

225

fucking truth. I love you, JJ. Fuck you and fuck me and fuck all of our fucking friends too.

Lynn

P.S. Please send me a copy of this play that everyone hates so much. Maybe in hate we find our answers right now.

Wednesday, February 22

Mrs. Lynn Towne
Room 809 West
Cedars Sinai Hospital
8700 Beverly Blvd.
Los Angeles, CA 90048

Lynnie,

Thanks. Here's the play. And here, too, Seattle—to the best of my ability . . . I guess it's time.

It was 18 months ago, hard as that may be to believe. August. Another day, another play. I stepped off the plane thinking I had landed in paradise. Lush green hills with waters flowing everywhere. Air clean and cool. I know the devil can come amid such splendor, but at the end of a smooth flight into another world I guess I had a momentary lapse in concentration. And then, I was also hoping for the best, which, translated, probably means I was ripe for a fall.

As arranged, my director met me at the airport.

"You're better-looking than your picture," she said.

And she smiled a curious smile. And we walked to her car.

As she drove up the freeway, Seattle sparkled in the distance. It was 9:00 at night and it was still light out. Buildings stood in silhouette against the mirror water of Puget Sound. The last ferries cut lines in the water's surface like diamonds leaving scratches on glass. People in cars made eye contact with us as we passed. There seemed to be no commercials between songs on the

227

radio. I breathed deeply and felt at ease. The world seemed at peace.

"Quite a response the other night when we read the play," the director said, her words slicing the air like a razor.

"In what way?" I asked.

"You'll see," I remember she answered.

And then we drove to the house I was supposed to stay in during my few days in town. Some friend of a friend was supposed to be there to let us in, but when we rang the bell there was no answer. And clearly there was no one inside. The house belonged to a woman who was a financial supporter of the theater and, at the moment, out of town. The whereabouts of the friend, who unfortunately hadn't left the key, were unknown. Being suspicious (or, as you'd say, paranoid) by nature, I thought this was a bad omen, and when my director seemed unable to make a decision about what to do next, I grew nervous about her as well.

"How about a hotel?" I asked.

"Don't be silly," she snapped.

But I wasn't being silly. I was tired from the flight and I wanted to have something to eat and lie down. The director, however, wouldn't hear of this. She had arranged a nice home for me to stay in and she wasn't about to deposit me in the local Holiday Inn. Instead, we drove all over the city for an hour and a half looking for this person with the key and I started to nod off in the front seat with a hangover headache from the airplane G&T's. Finally we ended up at the director's house, which she shared with three other women, and she actually offered me her own bed, seeing as they didn't have a couch.

"Where are you going to sleep?" I asked.

"I'll figure something out downstairs," she answered. "You go ahead, you must be exhausted."

This was beyond the truth. My eyelids were jet-lagged and falling fast. And I was irritated that no better arrangements had been made for my arrival. So I fought off a brief chivalrous impulse to say I'd take the floor and I fell into the bed, which turned out to be a foam mat on a wooden plank, not much different from the floor anyway. This doesn't bode well for the way my play's going to be treated, I remember I thought as I drifted off to a restless sleep.

In the morning I was greeted in the kitchen with dead cold silence by two of the director's roommates, who were Seattle butch in the extreme. I didn't know it, but my taking their roomie's bed out from under her had played right into everyone's advance expectations of me based on this reading that had already been held of my play. Seems the locals thought a play about women in business being cruel to other women was not going to make it big in Seattle. Especially when it was written by a man. Never mind that it was born of a true story. I was a pig for writing this play and my actions in the night now confirmed it. (Facts do seem to get me in trouble, don't they. . . .)

Later at the theater, actors, staff people, even technicians, greeted me with polite distance, as though they wanted me to know they would go ahead with the staged reading only because they had committed to it and I was there. The implication was that, had I not showed up, everyone would have been more than happy to call the whole thing off.

I proceeded with a torturous day of rehearsal in which actors mocked the characters they were playing, the artistic director of the theater stopped in to tell me he wouldn't have time to come to the performance that night, a lighting designer asked what the point of hanging any new spots was, and the stage manager said to the director with disgust in the middle of a scene I didn't want to cut, "Do

229

you realize this thing is going to play two and a half hours long?"

You know what that play was about, Lynnie. So did I, before I went up there. It seemed like a subject worthy of exploration to me. A woman is the first to break the sexual barriers to high positions in her field. She opens doors for other women who come in behind her, but they proceed to dispose of her because they have no use for the methods that were responsible for her success. The woman, whose sensibilities are hopelessly 60's, admittedly causes her own downfall by refusing to change with the times, but she is, nevertheless, treated with cruelty by the very women who are beneficiaries of her pioneering move into the field. Sixties idealism clashes with 80's practicality and, of course, the practical prevails. But not without a cost, some of which paints a slightly unflattering portrait, shall we say, of the new yupscale youth of today.

I expected some grief about that, but what these people at the theater didn't seem to realize was that my main character was not necessarily a mouthpiece for my own beliefs. The play was this woman's story, yes, because I felt she represented the passing of something, an old guard, I certainly hadn't intended her to become a Joan of Arc figure that would have to be burned at the stake to rid the world of a nagging conscience.

But the more the actors ridiculed her, the more I defended her. The more people laughed at the outdated sentiment that poured from her gut, the more I scowled in long-suppressed anger. The more she was perceived as ridiculous, the more I felt inclined to take her seriously. What was happening quickly became clear. I was barricading myself in to fight to the death for something I didn't even really believe in.

The evening's performance was then upon me, like an execution hour, while I, the play's prisoner, prayed in vain for a reprieve. But the doors opened, as they always do, and the theater quickly filled with fresh faces of the 80's. Clean scrubbed foreheads, navy skirts and blazers, and young-looking men with light-bulb-shaped haircuts showing skin around the ears. The smell of fresh leather briefcases and cologne wafted toward the stage. The actors, of course, picked up on the audience's mood right off the top and played everything for laughs. My heroine was turned into a buffoon to be pitied for clinging to the past, and the scummy little Eve Harringtons in the play came off as gallant saviors of the future. The story became a billboard for some work ethic I didn't even understand, and all subtlety disappeared beneath the leering smile of this strange ad's caricature. By the time it was all over, it was as though I had written a corporate comedy. The only thing left was for me to be introduced at the colloquium after the show as one of the herd so everyone could have their last laughs about the pitiful 60's and go home.

You can probably take it from there. . . Never one to pass up an opportunity to offend an audience, I proceeded not to reassure the gathered faithful but instead to harangue the little wimps for their empty-headed laughter. The more they smugly enjoyed themselves, I said right to their bulging eyes, the more pitiful they looked to me as human beings. I stared down this one girl with hornrims and a powder-blue double-breasted business suit and asked her if there was a minute in her day when the pursuit of money didn't fill her little being to the rim. "Sure," she answered, "about one o'clock, when my stomach starts to growl and I give Gracie's a call to check on the salmon."

Naturally this brought down the house. And the evening then went from bad to worse. I was reproached for having no sense of humor, like the character in my play, and I was viewed generally as pathetic, like any refugee of the 60's who actually believed the things that were said "back then." And to my surprise, by the time the potshots and sarcasm finally died down and everyone headed for their Saabs and BMWs outside, I began to agree with the little tight-asses. I *did* believe in the notions that this woman in my play had gone out on a fatal limb for. I *was* defending her by showing her downfall at the hands of others. I was, in fact, engaged in an identical struggle myself, with this play and others I had written. I *was* this figure, clinging stubbornly to an outdated sensibility, to a style of *theater* that had long since become passé. I was doomed, as she was, to fail. I, too, hadn't changed with the times. How could I not have seen this?

Now, left alone in the empty space of my heroine's arena, I knew it to be true. There is something about an abandoned theater with its cables, patch cords, lighting gels, and two-by-fours strewn about that brings you into direct contact with your soul. In the ugly glare of a bare-bulb worklight, words like "success" and "failure" take on an aura of black and white. Your dreams are either alive or dead. Your heart is either barren or full. You have either faced the truth and won or given in to deceit and become a victim of your own worst lines. There was no doubt where I sat at the moment. Even a roach on the floor turned its hind to me and walked away.

Later that night, at a motel down by the water (the director was more than happy to deposit me wherever I wanted now), I stared at my own reflection in a cheap mirror with fish decals around its wooden edging and thought about the first play I had ever written. *Arrival,* it was called. Big hit back at Michigan—remember, Lynnie? People all hyped from demonstrations on the Diag would fall into the theater at night and cheer its sense of energy and political awareness. I had synthesized a dramatic technique out of the electricity of commitment that was in the air all around me. I had felt how time could be grabbed and frozen as art. And how I would be cheered for this accomplishment if I could continue, as I had with this play, to make it feel as if I had understood, had experienced, had lived.

But now here I was in a damp motel room on Puget Sound. The days of triumph were long gone. For the third straight time, I had gone out with a play and failed. Only this time, it wasn't a matter of casting, or directing, or any coincidence of unfortunate timing. It was a matter of me. *I* had failed, even as myself. The fact that I had been working from true stories was of no consolation. My own story was a true story, like the subject of one of my plays, and no one was interested in hearing it either.

I went into the bathroom and swallowed an entire bottle of pills. The old Soma pills I always had on me. The downs we used to get so high on before we'd make delicious love in those afternoons that seemed to glow with the promise of a changed for the better future. I swallowed them all and called you, Lynnie, to tell you I loved you. You knew I was sad, that the play hadn't gone well, but you didn't know that you were saying a last good-bye. I couldn't tell you then and I couldn't tell you after I woke up twenty hours later either, the pills having only been up to knocking me out and leaving me with a pounding, wobbly headache, not putting me down, the way I intended, for the count. They were worn out too, Lynnie. I looked at the label and saw they had long since expired. And I could only laugh. Even my methods for putting myself out of my own misery were outdated. Not only could I no longer live off the past, I couldn't die off it either. I had to go on. I had to pick myself up and leave this moldy room and go home. To you. And to myself. Or what was left of me. And us.

I honestly thought I would tell you about it. I think I even started to a couple of times. But it came down to that old problem of voice for me, as usual. I had to find a form, a likeness, a sound. And I just couldn't. It's true I didn't speak for three months, but all that time I was

233

trying. I had to learn all over again, like a stroke victim or something. I had to start from scratch, feel my way through the darkness. Don't ask me why I didn't come to you for help. I guess I had to do this one on my own. I did finally manage to tell Deek about it. But by then I was already at work on this new play. And you and I had settled into an acceptance of the quiet. Maybe I was wrong, but I felt you wanted it that way too. You knew we were at a crossroads of some kind and I thought you were deciding which way to go and whether or not you still wanted me at your side. True?

The last year, then, I spent on this new play. And while I worked away in silence, you went away, I think, in fear. You stopped playing the piano the way I stopped speaking. I suppose neither of us had the nerve to face the sound of our hearts' own sorrow. Better to leave it unspoken than lay it out cold and shattered. It would have meant admitting to a failure of some sort, an end to our dreams and pledges to each other all those years ago. And this before either of us had any idea of what we would replace those dreams with. Our dreams took a long time to die, Lynnie. Longer than most, I'd say. And I don't think either one of us wanted to be the one to make the announcement.

But I did manage to write another play. And then Futterman came along. And the winter. I left you almost without a good-bye and fell into the sex of New York like an iron lonely for the fire. I'd found a way to speak again and, with it, a renewed desire to live. A new voice was there for real in a new play. And a new woman, whom I found myself undeniably attracted to, heard that voice for real in her ear. And she caressed it with that same welcoming warmth that you once did, Lynnie, when my sound was new, long waited for, and soothing to you. She claimed to have been waiting for it too. The same way you did all those years ago. And I, wanting to believe that

I could still arrive with such force in someone's life, with a voice that could say what someone had been waiting to hear, just spoke and spoke and reveled in the speaking.

But then half the rug was pulled out from under me. Futterman and the others ripped at the voice of the play and it was like they ripped part of my tongue out. And then I was back here, standing over the damage my new words had done to you, painfully aware that they had almost killed you, and I tried to speak to you with the stump that was left of this tongue in my mouth, and I hurt you even more, only to find that by the time I realized where I actually was, back here in our house, alone with an animal who could only look at me and wonder at what was going on, all there was left of me was, again, a silence. Just like before I left. I had come full circle. Back to nothing.

I tried to hold on to Andee. I even told you that was my plan. But I think I knew, even as I was speaking, that it was a lie. I was trying to convince myself. And it wasn't working. Whatever was left of this newly discovered voice was dissolving like an Alka-Seltzer into a bubbling gurgle in my own throat. By the time I finished that day, and you started screaming, and those nurses came in with the shot, I almost asked them if they would give it to me. I felt like I should be the one in that bed, not you. I despised myself. And yet all I could do was cry. Like a baby.

And I came home. And sat. And grew more and more afraid. Of what I had done. And maybe of what I still thought I might do. Seattle was back, Lynnie. The pills were right there in the medicine cabinet to send me straight to the damp motel room in the sky. And this time it would work.

But I saw that little package instead. And opened it. And found your music. And you. It had traveled from our house, where I now stood trembling, to New York City, where it bounced off Futterman the way I had, and now it was back here in our home, ready to be listened to, as if it was a key. To you. And to me. It had traced my own steps, Lynnie. And captured them as well. As I told you, my entire journey—our entire journey—was there for me. In song. And it spoke to me. And saved me. And demanded of me that I once again try to speak.

And I tried. And out came that croak. As well as all these paper words. It's a little better now, maybe. For a voice that's been lost so many times. But I don't think it's what it once was. And maybe, as you say, it shouldn't be. Maybe we have to speak to each other in our winter voices for a while. Or in new voices beyond those. Maybe we have to go on finding new voices forever. The way we once promised. With no regrets. And with lips sealed only by a kiss.

I feel like I'm saying what has to be said, Lynnie. And that we're getting at what has to be done. At what's had to be done for some time. I pray that my play speaks to you the way your music did to me. In a new way. And yet in a way that brings back some of the old. And I wait. This time for you to break the silence. My ears are open. As is my heart. For the first time in a long time, only for your voice, only for you.

All my love,
JJ

Thursday, February 23

Mr. J. J. Towne
8541 Coldwater Canyon
Los Angeles, CA 90056

Dear JJ,

You *have* spoken in a new voice. And its sound is music
to me too. I cried when I finished the play. And not
because I find it sad. But because you're so good. And
because you've persevered. And had the courage to recreate yourself, to rise, like the phoenix, from ashes. I had no
idea that all that had gone on up in Seattle. I understand
on some level, but I don't think I can forgive you for not
telling me. Knowing it now, and knowing what you went
through to write this year, I am happier for you than I've
ever been. And sadder for us. Because we were even
farther apart than I knew. And farther away from our love
than my mind can fathom.

But you're right when you say that I probably wanted it
that way too. I was looking at you and, as you say, trying
to decide, trying to imagine myself without you. And as
always, and in spite of the silence, the knowing crushing
in on itself silence, I couldn't see it. I felt we still belonged
to one another. Even if it meant we never smiled again.

Until you went to New York, that is. I knew the night
you called me and said you were going to stay that I had
lost you. I told Rudi. And I told myself. And I vowed that I
had to find a way back to myself, so that I could live,
alone if need be, and without you.

But I can't be alone, JJ. You know that. I sometimes
think that you have it in you to be a hermit, to go off in a
cave for years and live a totally satisfying existence. But I

237

need the warmth of touching. I can survive without a lot of things, but not that.

So, like you, I fell into my own desire and rediscovered it. I hadn't planned on it, to be honest. It just happened. But when I tasted its hunger again, I have to admit I went at it with a vengeance. And I need to feel that way, JJ. I need to like myself enough to want sex in that way. Because in sex I find everything. The present, the past, and, in the energy it gives me, a future.

And I think when I sensed that—that the future was there for me again—my music returned to me. Somewhere in there, between sensation and numbness, desire and denial, it lay in wait, ready to jump. I didn't plan on that either. I was sitting at home one night reading when I looked up and saw the piano as if it had suddenly returned from a long vacation. I went to it, said hello, lifted the lid, and began to play. It must have been like you finally sitting at your desk again and writing the first words of this play. Oddly wondrous and scary at the same time. But it flowed, JJ. And the more fucking I did, the more it flowed. Music—yours included—is connected to sex. I'm sure of it. We do hear bells when we have intercourse with another human being. They are the bells of our soul and whether they signal joy or pain, ecstasy or sorrow, they ring right on cue. Mine did. So did yours. We both wrote down the pattern. And then looked at it. And saw another pattern. The one in which we've been living our lives.

If my songs are a history of that pattern, JJ, then your play is a map of its discovery. You're writing here of a woman who would rather live on a park bench than within a life that has robbed her of her sexuality. It's no surprise that she gets raped. I feel, lying here in this bed, that I've been raped. Rape is the taking away of a woman's sex, or her right to it. It's the very subject of your play. And right at the heart of what's happened to us in our lives.

The play is wonderful, JJ. I don't care what any of

those schmucks say. You tell me your director had another job she wanted to take. Do you know your producer is going to China in the fall to put a TV cop in Peking? Let them all go to Peking as far as I'm concerned. Your play will survive, the way you've written it now, without any of them.

I want you back too, JJ. I have to tell you, I knew that even before. That's why I sent the tape to you in New York. And why I ran my car into the signpost up on the hill. Yeah, I did it myself. There *was* another car. But there's always another car. Just like there's always another woman. Or man. But it was you I wanted, and in the split-second when that guy came up on my right, I saw my opportunity and I took it. There was no running me off the road or even any loss of control. Only a quick mind and a reflex to match. I aimed for the post and I hit it. I didn't want to crack my head open but I did want to crack our lives open. Which, maybe with some help from the rest of this year, I did.

I hate the idea of you dying alone in a motel room up in Seattle, JJ. And of me putting myself through the windshield of a car just short of home. But that's what we've come to. I guess it's time to face it if we intend to move on. And I want to move on. As much as I've ever wanted anything in my life.

Your friend Deek has been writing a novel about a married couple who separate and then have an affair with each other to find their way back together. How about if we do some research for him, let him know how it would really feel? I'll warn you though. You have to be willing to have sex in unfamiliar places. Like theaters, restaurants, hotels. Or *hospitals*. Say, tomorrow night? Around 7?

You'll enjoy yourself. I promise.

And so will I.

Forever.
Lynn

Friday, February 24

Miss Andee O'Neill
c/o "Down by the River"
Warwick Studios
5460 Seventh Ave.
New York, NY 10020

Dear Andee,

Writing this letter is going to surprise me as much as I know reading it is going to surprise you. I wouldn't have guessed it would come from my hand, even by force. I wouldn't have guessed it would come from my heart, even if broken.

I'm going back with Lynn. I still love her. Maybe more than ever. Coming home and realizing how close I came to losing her has opened my eyes.

Not that they were closed while I was with you. I have to tell you, Andee, I love you too. I wouldn't give up the time I spent with you for anything. But you have to understand, it was, in a joyous way, time in a vacuum for me. I've told you a lot about myself, but not enough. It isn't that I deliberately kept any secrets from you. It's that I didn't tell you what I couldn't. What I wasn't able to say, even to myself, until I came back here.

I almost killed myself last year, Andee. I had reached the end of the tunnel with my plays and there was no light. I had seen the enemy and it was me. I was drained. Dead cold empty. Running on vapor. But somehow I scraped myself off the floor, rose up, and tried again. I wrote one more play. And it brought me to New York. And I was flying at the thought of having saved myself in the nick of time. It seemed like the supreme joke, because out of the blue I went from a reservation underground to one on Broadway.

And then there was you. Like a dream. Ready to see me all shiny new looking and clean. That was real, that current between us. If I saw you right now, it would still be there. But what wouldn't be there is that voice you told me about. The one you heard coming from me. And from way back in your life, from your own need. It isn't that you imagined it. Don't get me wrong. It's just that the one who whispered it wasn't really me. He used me, like a ventriloquist using a dummy, to give voice to something in the air. Something that was around me. For the first time in years. All this excitement, all this possibility, all this great white glistening hope. But I don't believe in hope, Andee. I never have. It's faith on discount to me and always seems to become a poor excuse for not being what we really should be. You almost made me believe God existed. You were that much of a gift to my life. But, seductive as the idea is—both of God and of me being with you—it doesn't really exist. And neither do I. Not as you know me.

So, I'm sorry. Even as a ghost in your life, I have to say good-bye. But I'll never forget you. I'll never forget that smile. And that feel of our first kiss. And last. I think you're better off for leaving Matt, so I won't apologize for getting you out on your own. If I can promise you anything, it's that that voice you've waited for does exist. It's out there somewhere. But not with him. And not with me. You'll find it. You've taken the first step. You'll see.

I wish you the absolute best. With all my heart. I'll miss you, Andee. My hand is trembling as I write this. The way it did when I first touched you. But good-bye.

Love,
JJ

Friday, February 24

Mr. Richard Case
27 Saltair Road
Malibu, CA 90233

Dear Deek,

I don't think this will come as any surprise to you. I'm
going back with JJ. If nothing else, this week here in
Insanitationville has given me time to think. To be sure of
what I really want. And I do want him, Deek. The minute
I saw his face again I knew. Maybe even before. I crashed
my car on purpose up there on the hill. A cheap theatrick, I
suppose, but it worked. He came to me. My anger's gone.
And he's mine again.

I know everything now. And not just about Miss
Soapstar. (I have to tell you, I watched her today and I'm
flattered in a way, at JJ's taste, in leaving her behind . . .)
But also about Seattle. And what JJ's really been going
through. I guess this year was an all-time low in terms of
sharing between us. But I think I understand his keeping
such desperation from me. And his telling you. And your
treating it as what it was—a confidence between best
friends.

You really are a special friend, Deek. Keeping intimacy intimate has to be one of the great talents. It's there
in your work. And also in your life. I thank you for not
telling JJ of our secret either. I was kind of expecting it
when I slammed the door in your face over here. But you
mean what you say, don't you? You like to try and keep
things what they really are. I know now that that isn't
easy, but I also know it's a struggle worthy of the best. I

242

feel a little bad for you in that I think it means you're destined to remain alone, except for brief excursions into the world of the flesh, such as ours. But I also envy you, at least slightly, for not having to witness the staleness that does always creep in. You've carved a solitary existence for yourself out there. But seeing it from the inside, as I feel I have now, I understand its benefits. And its peace.

You said after we made love that first afternoon that you didn't feel like it was our first time together. I didn't understand that then, but I think I do now. We've shared everything *but* our bodies over the years, haven't we? It actually feels more natural that we've gone ahead and done that too. And maybe it is possible to keep the experience in a special place. Like a chapter in a long story, the significance of which keeps changing with time as it finds its place in the whole. You taught me that the entire world can exist in a brief moment of time, Deek. Maybe that moment of time can then also find a way to go back out and exist as part of the world. If this is so, then we have become a part of each other's existence. We will always share possession of our moment together. But now we walk away from it, no more its owner than a clock is of time.

Thanks, Deek. I do feel like I've been gifted with something special, something to be savored, and that I've awakened all the better for it in the morning.

I think JJ and I are going to try and live out your novel. But why do I get the feeling that you already knew that . . . ?

I love you. As I always have. And now, as I always will.

Lynn

29 February

Mr. J. J. Towne
8541 Coldwater Canyon
Los Angeles, CA 90056

Dear JJ,

It's a strange day today, isn't it, the 29th of February? A day that doesn't even exist except for once every four years, in leap years, like this one. Next year the calendar will reach today and I'll look at it trying to remember all that happened way back when, and the day that it all happened on, or finished happening on, won't be there. Like us. We just won't be there. I keep telling myself that, repeating it like a psalm, but it won't sink in.

I do understand, I think. I've read your letter a thousand times trying to. I go over and over things, even hold the paper up to the light and try and see between all the lines. But what I'm looking for just isn't going to be there, is it? There's no way out, is there? No hope written in invisible ink that's going to miraculously appear once I find the secret key to make it show its face. You don't believe in hope. Or so you say.

But I think you do, JJ. I can accept that you're gone to me because I have to. But don't ask me to believe that there's no such thing as hope. They sell buttons over in the Village that say, "Since I gave up hope, everything is easier." Maybe that's more to the point. It hurts when you have hopes. Because with them come disappointments. But that's no reason to give up on them. You say the sound of your voice in my ear was that of a ghost. Maybe it was. The ghost of hope in your life, come back briefly

244

to haunt you. And to haunt me too. I made love to that ghost, JJ. I held it in my arms and it was warm. If that's what hope is, then I believe in it, I believe in ghosts. And I know you do too. Or did. At least for a moment.

I am glad Lynn is okay. And that you are too. Someone like you shouldn't kill himself, JJ. And someone like Lynn should live. In moments of weakness, I can't help but wonder what might have been if . . . But that's wrong. And not worthy of what we had. All I know is that Matt was involved in all that's happened in more ways than I think he'll ever know. And I'm sorry for that. But people like me who believe in hope also believe that things happen for a reason. Maybe it's all for the better. You found out what you really wanted and were lucky enough to get it back. I at least am free of Matt, which I agree I'm better off for. Now all I have to do is go on alone. Simple thing, right? So why is my hand shaking just to write the words? I guess it's something like what you had to go through to sit back down at your desk and try your hand at one more play. But you were right to do that, JJ. I still think the day will come when you see that. So maybe I'll be all right to have to do this. Maybe it's a question of practicing what I preach.

I love you, JJ. Be well. And be happy. Make your life what it deserves to be. And I'll try to do the same. I won't forget you, but I will forgive. It's a leap year for both of us. In a big way. I'm going to take this letter down to the post office now and watch them stamp it on the envelope for both our eyes to see. Proof that our day did exist, if only once in a great while. My heart to yours, JJ. Sealed with a kiss.

Andee

WESTERN UNION
LOS ANGELES 153 7000 6518 18333 18
1:00 P. Friday. 18 MAY

MR. J. J. TOWNE
C/O TRIBOROUGH REPERTORY
117 BROOME STREET
NEW YORK, NY 10012

CONGRATS, J. I READ FROM HERE YOU'RE A HIT. SAW A QUOTE FROM
DIANNE AIMSLEY SAYING YOU CAN'T DO A PLAY LIKE "THE WOMAN
ASLEEP" ON BROADWAY, AT LEAST NOT TO BEGIN WITH. OBVI-
OUSLY SHE'LL SETTLE FOR AN OBIE. FOR NOW. IMAGINE SO WILL
YOU. MAYBE GOOD THINGS DO COME TO THOSE WHO PLAY. I MEAN
WAIT. BEST ALWAYS. DEEK.

WESTERN UNION
NEW YORK CITY 413 201 400 17
3:15 P. Friday. 18 MAY

MR. J. J. TOWNE
C/O TRIBOROUGH REPERTORY
117 BROOME STREET
NEW YORK, NY 10012

JJ: CONGRATULATIONS AND ALL BEST WISHES ON SUCCESS OF "THE
WOMAN ASLEEP." PESTO ANYTIME. DOT AND RABBIT.

WESTERN UNION
New York City 146 178 143 31
5:01 P. Friday. 18 May

MR. J. J. TOWNE
C/O TRIBOROUGH REPERTORY
117 BROOME STREET
NEW YORK, NY 10012

DEAR JJ. MY HEARTFELT CONGRATULATIONS AND BEST WISHES FOR
YOU AND "THE WOMAN ASLEEP ON THE LIBRARY BENCH." YOU
ARE A FINE WRITER AND MOST DESERVED OF THIS SUCCESS AND
JUDGING FROM YOUR REVIEWS AND THE ATTENTION THE PLAY IS
GARNERING HERE IN NEW YORK A MOVE TO BROADWAY WOULD
NOT BE OUT OF THE QUESTION. OF COURSE I WOULD STILL BE
INTERESTED IN PARTICIPATION SHOULD YOU AND TRIBOROUGH REP
FIND YOU WOULD LIKE TO GO IN THIS DIRECTION. SUSIE JOINS
ME IN AGAIN WISHING YOU OUR BEST. FONDLY. PETER FUTTERMAN.

WESTERN UNION
Los Angeles 8899 9255 1137 103
8:10 P. Friday. 18 May

MR. J. J. TOWNE
C/O TRIBOROUGH REPERTORY
117 BROOME STREET
NEW YORK, NY 10012

SO HOPE LIVES. YOU TOOK THE TOWN AFTER ALL. CONGRATULA-
TIONS, JJ. NOBODY'S HAPPIER FOR YOU THAN ME. LOVE ALWAYS.
ANDEE.

WESTERN UNION
Los Angeles 1888 16130 1202 43
11:51 P. Friday. 18 May

MS. LYNN TOWNE
C/O TRIBOROUGH REPERTORY
117 BROOME STREET
NEW YORK, NY 10012

WELL I GUESS THIS MEANS YOU'LL BE STAYING THERE A WHILE
LONGER. DON'T BLAME YOU. IN FACT I ENVY YOU. BUT YOU KNOW
THAT. PLEASE CONGRATULATE JJ. DOES THIS MEAN THAT YOU
WON'T BE MARRYING ME? THAT YOUR HUSBAND WILL HAVE TO
WRITE ANY FILM WE PRODUCE? THAT YOU CAN FALL IN LOVE WITH
THE SAME PERSON TWICE? THAT WE REALLY SCREWED UP BY LET-
TING THE CASE NOVEL GO TO THE GUYS ACROSS TOWN? SAY YES
TO ANY OR ALL OF THE ABOVE AND YOU'RE FIRED. AS ALWAYS. OR
ALWAYS AS. DAVID.

Sunday, May 20

Mr. Richard Case
27 Saltair Road
Malibu, CA 90233

Dear Deek,

Thanks for the telegram. You hear right. It's really happening for me, man. I'm everywhere. Press, radio, parties, magazines. Still won't touch TV, which pissed off the PR lady at the theater, but I have my limits, what can I say? That it was worth the wait? No, I can't say that. I'd give you the last few years without so much as a flinch. That it's as exciting as I used to imagine? No, sorry, but I guess I've been disappointed a time or so too many to go clicking my heels up Broadway. That it's made me happy? Sorry to spoil a straight, but the answer to this is an unqualified yes. I'm not running around feeling too full of myself or anything, but I have to admit my eyes are smiling when I brush the pearly whites in the morning.

Lynn and I have this terrific little place in Chelsea. 23rd Street just off Ninth. White shutters, flower boxes, even a clean stoop to sit out on in the evening. The sublet runs through October, so we have the city at our feet and nowhere we have to go. And we're loving it. And each other. I wouldn't have believed it was possible, Deek, but we've fallen hard for one another all over again. We read each other poetry and talk well into the night. We go for long walks, we shop, and fall for everything in sight. We make love two and three times a day and the more I get of her, the more I want. She tastes like a baby and I feel like a suckling pig. I don't know if it's like your book, but I do

250

know it's good. And that I'm grateful she's mine. By the way, when do we get to read this book anyway? Lynn tells me you sold it to the movies and someone's scripting it before it's even seen the light of day.

I talked to Andee the other night. She's out in LA now (that's one thing about irony—it never quits, does it?) and she sent me a telegram after the reviews hit the fan. The old heart kind of fluttered at the sound of her voice, but the temptation was honestly gone. Maybe you should look her up. She's trying to make the jump to the big screen and I'm sure she'd be happy to get the call.

You know, there's also something I keep meaning to ask you about. I wake up in the night, think of it, and then promptly forget come morning. You never told me about this affair you were having with the married woman. I guess Lynn and I really closed up shop on you after she got out of the hospital. We weren't even answering the phone there for a while. But what happened? I always wanted to know. If you don't want to write about it, just give me a signal, and I'll go somewhere and give you a call.

That's the scoop, Jack. The talk of the town. I'm smooth and carefree. Got my woman and she's got me. Got a play running into the night. Don't even mind the hard morning light. Think of you out there by the big blue sea. But I'm glad I got Manhattan and Manhattan's got me.

Take good care, buddy. Thanks for being there for me. This year and always.

JJ

Sunday, May 20

Mr. David Raskov
DR Productions
The Burbank Studios
Producers 11, Suite 6B
Burbank, CA 91505

Dear David,

How nice to hear you speak of envy, such a base human emotion for you to be experiencing. Maybe *all* of us will come out of this year the better for having lived. . .

     Yes, JJ and I have fallen in love again. Yes, that means I won't be marrying you. And yes, we screwed up to let the Case book go across town. Especially because JJ could have written it from the inside out. But that's the movies, isn't it? Why should people who are intimate with a story be the ones to bring it to the screen when there are others around who can accomplish the task with total indifference? Even the author was attracted to the package over there because he knew no one involved and those he did speak to had not the slightest interest in his view of the story as a film. I get the impression he wanted to let go of this one. . .

    New York is wonderful. I always said the only way to do this town was with great wealth or great love inside you. I feel like a schoolkid on summer vacation. Our apartment is just right. An adorable little place downtown, not too expensive, and within a short walk of everything we need. Haven't been near a car *or* an anxiety attack since we arrived. It's a little odd sleeping in someone else's bed after all these years, but along with everything else it's added to the sense of starting fresh. And unfamiliar sheets can make for unfamiliar (i.e., terrific) sex. (Yes, lust can be restored once lost . . . and yes, within marriage. . .) Even Rudi seems to have picked up on this. She has three dogs on the block waiting for her to come out every morning and I've noticed a little bounce in her step that hasn't been there in years. Maybe you *should* consider moving the office here, David. We could call it Old Dogs Learn New Tricks Productions. . .

The successful playwright sends his best, as do I. Hope you're able to turn the lights on and off there without me. I'll keep my eyes open for the next story we can lose to our good friends and associates around us. (Did you ever think of officially designating us as a finder company? At least that way we could take a fee for our contribution to the process.)

Take care, David. And if you're worrying about keeping our expenses respectable, think how easy it's going to be to run up the phone bill with me on the other side of the world.

As always,
Lynn

253

3 AM, a steamy night in New York City, and I just awoke from a dream of a red notebook lying in a gutter misplaced. I suppose that's a significant dream, seeing as the notebook was this notebook, my notebook, the one I began earlier this year, when I feared I myself had been misplaced. I haven't thought of it much since leaving the hospital back in March—I guess I've been too busy living—but it occurred to me lying there in bed that as long as it had jumped into my consciousness, then maybe I ought to take a look at it. Maybe it would trace the amazing story of the second coming of JJ's and my love and I could sit and revel in it over a cup of tea out here in our Chelsea kitchen. It would all be there on paper, from the disenchantment and total despair of a deserted heart to the elation and discovery of passion renewed. An amazing story that even a sound sleeper would love to get up in the middle of a night to read.

So I went to my suitcase at the back of the closet and, without awakening JJ, slid the spiral from the zippered pocket in which it has rested untouched all these months, and I tiptoed out here to the kitchen, put up some water, and prepared myself for my midsummer night's surprise. But what do I find? My story, with its ups and downs, its secret joys and affairs, the history of nothing less than the most tumultuous year of my life? Hardly. Instead, there are but a few pages hinting at confusion, fear, anger, sex, and a floundering soul's unanswered questions. Nothing

254

at all of the epic journey I feel I have made to this place where I now rest, where I lie with my husband, once again in total harmony and peace. Reading a notebook or journal is, I think, something like looking at films of people making love. It appears attractive only insofar as it engages the imagination and hints at the inner drama that is, in truth, being lived. Otherwise the feel is pornographic, which is to say, deficient, superficial, or preoccupied with surface detail. The life of the heart is so much more, you feel, than an account of how you spent your days.

Earlier tonight, JJ and I watched fireworks from a terrace overlooking Central Park. At one point I turned away from the flaring skyrockets and drifting trails of dying light only to see that JJ was crying. A tear fell slowly down the left side of his face and it turned purple, then red, then green with the pyrotechnics in the night. I stared at it until JJ caught sight of my gaze and turned away. I pulled him back and smiled. No one else knew, but this was a picture of the happiest man in New York City. It took years for this tear to be illumined in such light. Years for us to reach this moment in which we could stand there, high above the streets, breathe deeply, and afford to cry. I kissed JJ. I kissed the wetness all over his face and devoured it as though it was come. Much has been written about oral sex in our time, but no one to my knowledge has explained the pleasure in swallowing a lover's tears. There was sorrow in them, but also the joy of release, the salt of sweat and agonized waiting, and the fire of triumph long deserved. I never loved my husband more than when I swallowed those tears. They had come of his struggles and they belonged inside of me as surely as they had flowed from inside of him. This was the opposite of pornography. This was the truth of love.

Later, when the fireworks were over and we arrived back here at home, we called Deek on an impulse and sent a three-way silence into the long-distance American night. Very little was spoken but a great deal was said. Not one of us, I suppose, could possibly fathom the infinity of connections between us. It seemed fitting that a satellite was required to bounce our heaving breaths and smiling sighs from ear to ear to ear. If any of us was closest to understanding, though, to intuiting the exact qualities in our quiet, it had to be me, who had been to bed with everyone on the line, who had listened to such silences in these men and in myself with the only distance separating mouth from ear being the thickness of a lip.

I thought about this while we sat there on the phone, and again later when JJ and I were making love. Somehow when JJ was inside me, Deek was there too. It was as though sensation in this moment was intensified by all that made it possible, including the jumble of events that led JJ and me through our frozen winter and thawing spring to the heat of this summer bed. If JJ's affair with his actress had been about finding his voice, then mine with Deek had been about giving that voice body. Just as a play's language is released only in its actual speaking, our love was reborn only when circumstances again united us in physical sex. JJ was again inside me. But in returning my body to me, and with it my desire, Deek had put him there. It was as though he had created this moment; had, in fact, created us, however indirectly, in this new incarnation of our love.

I fucked JJ. And then fucked him some more. I can't seem to get enough of him these days. We really did live out Deek's scenario of the married couple having an affair in the big city, public trysts included. My favorite one, I think, was over at the South Street Seaport, where we did it against a rotting wooden breaker beneath one of the old piers. The wood was damp and musty and its smell reminded me of the canyon back home after a rain. When JJ pushed my bare legs against it, I guess I felt about as decadent as I have in my life. Tonight, though, it was lace curtains and chintz in a Chelsea brownstone and Rudi sighing at our feet. Little family on the bed, we call it. And that about says it all.

Now JJ sleeps in the next room and I sip tea over scribblings in a notebook that came to me in a dream. Which is what the events of this year now look like to me even as I stare at the bony traces of their hard reality on these crinkly pages. Funny, but that's what we still seem to long for even in all our modern sophistication. The more seriously we take the world and the more we demand that it change in our own image, the more we beg it to exist as in a dream. All I know is, at the moment I have mine. JJ is at peace with himself. The world knows he's a writer, and a good one at that. My music pours from me in droves. And our bills are paid and more. Maybe notebooks do tell the truth. In their own fragmented way. Tonight my red one records a dream within a dream. I'm going to take it back in the other room now. And put it back where it came from. And get back in bed where I came from. And hope against hope that the dream I've recorded here is one from which I never wake up.

5th of July

Mr. J. J. Towne
351 West 23rd St.
New York, NY 10011

Dear JJ,

I was just out walking on the beach and the burnt-out stumps of firecrackers and collapsed ashes of pinwheels and snakes that are scattered through the sand from the fireworks last night somehow reminded me of us this year, and I came in to tell you. It's not a sad feeling I have; just a spent one. The book's done and I've made all my deals. They've got a script already at the studio and are casting the film. I'm in that wonderful phase where I'm counting the bucks without even having been reviewed. And all this before the damn thing is even published. The world just keeps getting farther and farther ahead of itself. Seems like before too much longer there'll be no need for the present to exist at all. Only the future and our expectations of it, which we will have become. I'm lazy today. But with a smile on my face.

I also have a very interesting dinner to tell you about. (Can't put hunger in the future . . .) I was lying around the other day making best friends with my in-between bottle (the one that keeps me company through these in-between, i.e., nonwork, phases) when the phone rang and who should be on the line but the fallen angel herself, your visiting friend from the east, Miss Andee O'Neill. She was very sweet, the way she introduced herself, saying she was a good friend of yours and had heard a great deal about me from you and was in town, etc., and would I be free to get together sometime for lunch or a drink? To be honest, I hesitated. I feel like we all did spring cleaning on the whole affair, and you know me—when it comes to stuff like this, I like to draw my lines clean. But something in that voice of hers did it, J. I think you once described it as breathing silk, an apt description if I do say so myself, and there was just no way I was going to deny my ears the experience of such a caress live. I said I don't do lunch, that meals in the midday sun don't sit well with me, and suggested dinner if she was free. Her laugh told me she was, and before I knew it I was pulling the old Armani from the closet and shaking my head in disbelief.

I took her to The Ivy, thinking it would be a treat to watch her devour one of their whipped cream concoctions for dessert, and I have to say I was not disappointed with the evening's sights. Much to my delight, she frowned at all the blackened redfish and Cajun chic and ordered a steak blood rare, and at dessert picked the chocolate chocolate chocolate cake with the whipped cream and suggested that we share. I don't know when I've ever enjoyed more the simple passing back and forth of a fork. She does focus on the mouth, as you said many a time, but I wasn't quite prepared for the fact that this would include hers as well as my own. Without wishing to provoke you toward relapse or anything, I'll just say that my dick took a beating trying to find a way to coexist with my pants.

We talked about you, of course. She had questions to ask as well as things to tell. All of it good, I might add, and very consistently in the past tense. She's honestly happy for the way your life has worked itself out and she's content, if not thrilled, with being out here on her own for the time being. She looks back on the time with you as a big boost in her belief in herself and she honestly doesn't think she'd have had the nerve to leave Stanese and go for the movies if it hadn't been for you. Nothing much has come her way yet in terms of work here, but she isn't worried about that, she knows it'll happen. Which brings me to the funny part of the evening. Or, if not funny, the part that made me decide I had to write you and tell you all this.

After we finished eating, we took a walk down Robertson and looked in windows at furniture, antiques, the latest from design town—you get the drift . . . It was nice in that objects became, as often as not, excuses to talk about ourselves, our likes and dislikes, and where they've come from over time. I heard about her childhood up in Boston and she heard about the Lincoln Continentals and mansions and what it's like to choose to become a writer and fall from grace (at least temporarily). When we decided it was impossible to say which was worse—having everything and losing it or having nothing and wanting everything—she turned to me and I saw a tear fall from her eye. She tried to say it was nothing, but after we walked back up the street, got into my car, and made it most of the way back across town, she finally told me what I think the purpose of the evening, the purpose of her calling me in the first place, was probably about.

Seems she was over at MGM for an audition a couple of weeks ago, when she heard about my book and the film of it that was in the works. So she got ahold of a script and had her agent get her a reading with the film's director. How could they resist her, she thought, for the part of the girl our husband has his serious fling with before going back to his wife when, for all she knew, she *was* this character, or at least the real-life person on whom the character was based? She didn't know the details but she knew it was my book and she says she recognized you in the character of the husband, so how could the girl *not* be her?

So she gets herself together and goes in and does a great reading and the director absolutely flips for her. He keeps her there for two and a half hours and doesn't even

260

ask her to dinner at the end of it (i.e., he's serious). He even arranges a screen test with the lead they're thinking of using. In short, he does everything but tell her the part is hers and then sends her home to wait by the phone.

Well, a day passes. And then another. And then she gets a call from the producer, who asks her if she'd mind coming back in one more time. She doesn't know what's going on, but she goes. And when she gets there, the director and producer usher her in to see some studio VP who is so new to his job that the furniture in his office still has tags on it. And he just sits and stares at her for a good ten minutes without saying a word. She's never felt more like a piece of meat in her life, but what can she do, she just sits there squirming along with the producer and director.

Finally, the veep stands from his requisition desk and goes over to his requisition VCR, where he runs through her test on a monitor at double speed with no sound and then turns back to Andee, shakes his head, and says he's sorry, no man alive would leave *her* to go back to his *wife*.

Well, the director protests and the producer protests but Andee knows the matter is closed. When one of them says that leaving someone like her could prove only that the husband's love for his wife must be genuine, she thanks them all, excuses herself, and leaves.

Then I guess it was a few days with her own in-between bottle before she finally picked up the phone and dialed me. Now, sitting in my car parked outside her apartment, she finishes telling me all this and somehow manages a laugh. At first I think she's forcing it and that it's going to turn into tears again if I so much as open my mouth. But then I see that the laughter is genuine, that before me sits a woman, not a girl, who has been burned by love and has managed to break through to the essential irony of living, which more often than not comes with many more years and experiences than she has any right

261

to call her own, which usually whispers to you nastily in the cold dark of further down the line nights, that pain qualifies you for nothing, only more living.

I looked at her, JJ, and I have to tell you that in that moment I was totally in love. Or as close to it as someone who has just seen the true face of love modulating back and forth in its performance masks of tragedy and comedy could be. I'm crazy, I know. I spend my life conjuring things and then fall helpless before the power of my own creations. I live by my imagination and then imagine myself right out of the possibilities of my own living. I told you that this year I had fallen into something with a married woman. Well, I can tell you now that she was but a fiction. I made her up. And then fell hard for her. So I then made up a way to get rid of her. And as you went out into the world and lived, you sent someone to me in words who then showed up in the flesh only to be told she was overqualified to portray herself in the story about her that I had written. And now here she was in front of me. I had broken bread with her, listened to her voice, spoken to her, touched her. She was now laughing in the face of her own love just as I had done countless times before her. And this was making me love her. So what did I do? I walked her to her door, watched helplessly as she kissed my cheek, and listened as both our hearts wondered aloud at the strangeness that I should be standing there in her hallway in Los Angeles instead of you. What could I say except good night?

Now, as I write to you, send these words from my world to yours, I wonder at the complexities of my own heart. I, who like to keep my house in order, invent whatever is necessary to fill the void, am baffled. How can a fictitious character compete with a living, breathing human being for the race of my pulse? Even for someone who believes in the power of the written word, isn't this a bit much? But then again, who am I to call something or someone "fiction" or "real" in the first place? Who is to say that I'm any more "real" than the stories I invent? I know I laid with my character this year and loved her fully. I've never had better sex with anyone in my life. We came together without so much as laying a hand on one another. We talked into the night to the point where each of us unzipped our soul. I defy anyone to tell me that such a dialogue isn't real. It would be like saying that at this very moment I am not conversing with you.

You know this as well as I do, JJ. It's nothing new to you. Your excursion into New York this year turned into an excursion into your own heart which then turned into a new version of your play which then gave you the streets of New York. I wouldn't want to draw the lines between fiction and reality there either. The fact is, in matters of the heart, the essence of the drama always exists between the lines. The truth of our declarations are always spoken offstage. The ups, the downs, the mad dashes for safety in the night can be strung together, but only after the fact. Love letters written with an eye to the future reveal their hidden truths only when read looking back toward the past. Like the painting that froze you that night on the sidewalk outside Toll, I am frozen now by these very words I see before me. But I feel so grateful for them at the same time. So alive. I guess it's like you said, it is only when the boundaries of color are stripped bare that we sense the aliveness of our own sight.

And somehow all the boundaries were stripped bare for me in that hallway after my dinner with Andee O'Neill. Everything that had passed between all of us this year was present in the sound of her voice. The excitement of anticipation, the sensuality of a first touch, the knowing glance of false expectation, the after-the-fact regret of passing time. When she finished the story about being turned down for the part of herself, I was tempted to play God and intervene. It occurred to me that I could pick up the phone and scotch the whole deal unless the jerks guaranteed her the role. But something stopped me. I didn't want to be God. I didn't want to break that barrier for her which, from my point of view, separated her more from her past than her hopes for the future.

"You walked away from your past in coming out here," I said to her. "It's probably better that you don't go back."

I know she agreed with me too. I finally got to see the neon smile. Then she asked me inside. And I said no. For me, a line drawn is a line respected. I said good night and privately cherished the small kiss on my cheek.

Outside my heels sounded very loud on the pavement as I returned to my car. Kind of a hyped-up revelation of character that such walks always seem to advertise even if only to one's own tortured soul. I got in, shut the door on my own silence, and stared at myself in the rearview mirror. I had turned down sleeping with this woman, this embodiment of physical beauty, for the sake of my inner peace of mind. Now she would remain where she belonged to me, mixed with story and truth in a way that left everything in its place, everyone—real or not—in their time. I would not be the voice she longed for either, JJ. Such voices, to me, must come from within, where the heart alone can decipher them.

Instead, I drove home, the now familiar drive, which left me at my desk, with my own voices, the ones that arrive in letters, or out of the night, or as the sun sinks warmly into a late afternoon sea. In such a place, at the end of such journeys, such voices become the challenges to reality that memories often are. In such places, a writer can be happy. For in such places, fiction will, by definition, always have the last word.

Love to you both. I think all in our story sleep happily tonight.

Deek